THE
DEATH

THE SECOND DEATH

KEL RICHARDS

OM
publishing

Copyright © Kel Richards 1993

First published in the U.K. 1996
by arrangement with Hodder Headline (Australia) Pty Limited

02 01 00 99 98 97 96   7 6 5 4 3 2 1

OM Publishing is an imprint of Paternoster Publishing,
P.O. Box 300, Carlisle, Cumbria CA3 0QS U.K.

Scripture quotations in this publication are taken from the
GOOD NEWS BIBLE Copyright © 1966, 1971, 1976
by The American Bible Society, N.Y.

British Library Cataloguing in Publication Data

A catalogue record for this book is available from the British Library.

ISBN 1–85078–179–6

Typeset in Australia by G.T. Setters Pty Limited
Printed in Great Britain by Cox & Wyman Ltd., Reading

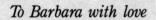

To Barbara with love

Author's Note

This is a work of fiction. Any resemblance between any fictional persons, or radio stations, portrayed in this book and any living persons, or radio stations, is purely coincidental.

Chapter 1

'Kill the bastard!'

Mark Roman groaned inwardly at the venom in the voice then rumbled into the microphone.

'A touch harsh, perhaps?'

'It's what he's done! It's what he deserves! Kill him I say.' It was a male voice, perhaps middle-aged, and fierce with anger.

'Let me ask you this,' said Roman to the caller, 'If you were offered the job of official hangman, if you were invited to pull the lever on the trap, to do the actual killing—would you do it?'

'Too right I would! Too right. Wouldn't hesitate.'

When there was a particularly grisly murder in the headlines the open-line callers on Roman's radio talk-back show always raised the issue of capital punishment.

'And after you'd taken his life,' continued Roman, 'how would you be any different to him? Wouldn't you be a killer too?'

'Don't be stupid. Legal killing isn't murder.'

'No, it isn't murder, quite right. But it is still killing. Still taking of a human life.'

'A life for a life,' persisted the caller, 'that's the law.'

'What law?'

'Well. . . it's in the Bible isn't it?'

'What you're referring to is the *lex talionis*.'

'Now you're showing off, Mr Roman. Those are probably the ony two words of Greek you know.'

'Latin.'

'Eh?'

'Not Greek, Latin. And yes, I only know half a dozen words of Latin, and those are two of them. I can tell you what they mean too—the law of revenge. And the *lex talionis*, or law of revenge, in the Old Testament doesn't grant a right, it imposes a limit. It means that if you want to be so bloodthirsty as to take revenge, then your revenge for one murder is limited to one killing. It was intended to prevent endless series of "pay-back" killings—the sort of thing that used to happen in tribal societies. One life for one life: it's an upper limit, that's all.'

'Well I only want to kill one person: the bastard who committed the murder that was in the news tonight. He's an animal. Worse than an animal. He deserves to die. And if they ask me to do the honours, I'd be proud.'

'You sound passionate about it?'

'Too right I am! Too right!'

'Then perhaps it's a good thing our legal system is based on rational thought and not on passion,' said Roman as he closed the phone fader on the console and hit the cart button to fire off a music sting. Three sharp brass chords punctuated the program, and then Roman's voice continued with a time call and a station ID after which he pointed to Peter Stanley his panel operator to play a commercial break.

While the ads were playing Roman sorted through the papers scattered over his studio desk and found the weather forecast.

These were the things the amateurs couldn't do. So many radio stations these days believed that talk-back shows could be hosted by politicians, or politicians' wives, or ex-politicians, or ex-politicians' ex-wives. Roman thought of them as amateurs because no matter how opinionated and talkative they were they had few radio craft skills.

They never remembered to tell the time, or identify the station, or themselves. And if they did the weather forecast they made a meal of it.

'After this,' Peter's voice crackled over the intercom, 'fifteen seconds.'

The commercial break ended and Roman's voice resumed its mellow patter.

'This is the Mark Roman Talk Back Show and. . .'

To his left line eight on the open-line board was flashing, and the computer screen in front of him told him that the caller on line was named Liz: 'She wants advice' his producer had typed.

'. . .and Liz is next. Good evening Liz, welcome to the show.'

As he spoke, Roman pressed the line eight button and opened the phone fader on the console.

'Is that you Mark?' asked the female voice on the phone line.

'Yes it is.'

'I have a problem, Mark'—the voice had an emotional and breathy quaver to it— 'and I was hoping that you could give me some advice.'

'Well, I'll try. What's the problem?'

11

'It's to do with my son...my nephew.'

'Well, which is it: your son or your nephew?'

'It's Simon actually.'

'And Simon is...?'

'My stepson I suppose I should say. It's a bit confusing.'

'Just take a deep breath and explain it slowly so none of us get confused.'

'Simon is my sister's son. And when she died—my sister that is, Simon's mother—we adopted him.'

'You and your husband?'

'Yes, that's right.'

'That was a very kind thing to do.'

'Oh, well. Anyway, that was a long time ago. Simon's grown up now. He's out of university and started work...' The voice, someone in their sixties, started to develop a sobbing note. '...and I'm worried...I'm getting very worried...'

'It's Simon that you're worried about,' interrupted Roman, giving his caller a chance to pull herself together. 'So tell us, Liz, why you're worried about him.'

'I'm sorry,' said the voice on the phone with a snuffle, 'I'm all right now.' There was a pause and then she said, 'I'm worried that his father is trying to steal him back again.'

'His father is still alive? I assumed that when you said your sister had died and you had adopted this boy...'

'His father is not an Australian,' interrupted Liz. 'He's a foreigner. And I'm very worried now, and so is my husband too, that he might be trying to steal Simon back again.'

'What contact has he had with Simon while you've been bringing him up?'

'Oh, none! None at all. I've seen to that.'

'Why? Why this desire for the boy to have no contact with his father?'

'Oh Mark . . . It's very hard to explain . . . especially on radio. But if you knew the circumstances. If you knew what had happened.'

'Tell us what happened then.'

'I don't think I can. Not on the radio. Can you just believe me that there were good reasons why his father shouldn't have any contact with Simon—'

'Did a court say that?'

'Oh yes! We adopted Simon legally. In this country. And Simon's father had a lawyer in court but we were given custody.'

'How long ago did all this happen?'

'Seventeen years Simon has lived with us, ever since he was five.'

'So he's twenty-two now?'

'That's right. And now his father is back in the picture again. Making another attempt,' she started to sob again as she said this.

'But Simon is an adult now,' said Roman. 'There can be no question of claiming custody.'

'No . . . no . . . that's not it. He's South American, you see.'

'Who's South American?'

'Simon's father. And you know how hot blooded these South Americans are.'

'You talked about him trying to "steal" Simon. You don't mean kidnapping, do you?'

'Oh, no. At least I don't think he'd do that.'

'So what do you mean by "steal"?'

'He wants to get Simon on his side. To turn him against us.'

Roman started to worry that this call was becoming

13

confusing to most of his listeners. He had to intervene before they became bored and changed stations.

'Look, Simon is an adult, right?' rumbled Roman, in his softest, deepest voice.

'Yes,' quavered Liz.

'He's lived with you and your husband for seventeen years?'

'Yes.'

'Does he love you?'

'Oh, yes! He's a very affectionate boy.'

'Then you have nothing to worry about. If this middle-aged South American turns up there is no way he will be able to alienate your stepson's affections. Even if they establish friendly contact. Simon's childhood belongs to you, and no one is going to be able to "steal" him away from you. So stop worrying about it.'

'If you say so,' Liz's voice on the telephone sounded doubtful.

'I do say so. Stop worrying. And thanks for your call.'

'Good night.'

Roman slid the phone fader closed and hit the disconnect button near his left hand. As he did so he told the time, picked up a slip of paper in his right hand, and rattled off the weather forecast. Then he pointed to Peter for another bracket of commercials.

Roman clicked off his own mike switch and pressed the intercom button.

'Call the newsroom Peter,' he said, 'and take the news heads off the end of this break.' Peter nodded in response.

The commercials and the news headlines together gave Roman a three minute break—time enough to make a cup of coffee. He pushed himself to his feet and hurried out of the studio.

He was a tall man, broad shouldered and solidly built. Although he was not fat, just solid, he had the heavy, flat-footed walk of a much fatter man.

The radio station's tiny kitchen was located conveniently close to the studio. All radio programs, thought Roman as he put instant coffee, sugar and milk into the bottom of a mug, run on coffee. He filled the mug with boiling water from the urn and hurried back to the studio, stirring the coffee with a plastic spoon as he walked.

As he re-entered the studio the news reader was wrapping up the headlines. That meant Roman had about twenty seconds to get behind the desk ready to take over. But years of experience in radio had taught him that twenty seconds was enough, and he didn't hurry.

'The next full news bulletin will be at twelve o'clock,' said the voice of the reader, from the news studio at the other end of the building.

At these words, Roman flicked open his mike and said, 'And that's exactly twenty-eight minutes from now. Good evening—Mark Roman with you until midnight, and if you'd like to call there are some lines available on the board right now...'

The usual patter that kept the show running smoothly fell fluently from his lips while his eyes were checking out the computer screen and his hands were pressing a button and opening a fader.

'George is next,' rumbled the deep voice that had made Mark Roman famous. 'Good evening, George.'

'Evening, Mark. Look, you were a bit tough on that bloke earlier.'

'What about?'

'About the death penalty.'

'I take it you're in favour of capital punishment George?'

'You bet your life I am,' came the insistent reply, sizzling over the telephone wire.

Roman sighed inwardly, and said, 'Tell me why, George.'

'Well, it's obvious Mark. I'd always thought you were an intelligent bloke and could understand the obvious.'

'George, I'm giving you the right to spell out the "obvious" for us.'

'These people are a menace to society, right?'

'By "these people" you mean murderers?'

'Right. Anyone who commits a brutal murder, like the one that happened today, is a menace to society. So they should be put out of the way.'

'Locking them up will do that, surely?'

'Not permanently it won't. If there was a dog in your street that behaved like this murderer did, you'd have the dog put down—right?'

'If a dog was vicious and attacked people I certainly think it should be put down.'

'Right. Same principle. The bloke who did this murder is just a vicious dog. And he should be put down like any other vicious dog. Right?'

'No. I'm afraid that's where you and I part company, George. Because this murderer—any murderer—is not a dog. A person who commits a murder is still a human being, and to equate them with dogs and treat them like dogs is surely to sink down to their level.'

'Well I'm glad you've got all this bleeding heart compassion for murderers. It's just a pity, Mark, that your compassion doesn't extend to the victims,' rasped

16

the caller, lashing himself into a fury that dripped with sarcasm.

'You're the one who lacks compassion for victims, George,' growled Roman, letting an edge of anger creep into his voice.

'No, I'm the one who wants to save future victims by disposing of murderers.'

Roman took a deep breath, and then said more calmly, 'Let's go back to basic principles, George.'

'What principles?'

'Capital punishment violates three basic principles: justice, mercy and compassion.'

'How do you figure that out?'

'Justice: because our legal system is imperfect and will occasionally make mistakes. If you lock up someone by mistake you can set them free. If you execute someone by mistake—well, it's too late.'

'I'll take that risk. Better to execute a few innocent people than let murderers walk the streets.'

'As long as you're not one of the innocent people who gets executed, eh, George?'

'Eh?'

'Mercy: because as long as someone is serving a long prison sentence for murder there is always the chance they will repent of what they have done, and turn to God, and to the family of the victim, and ask for forgiveness.'

'I wouldn't forgive them!' snapped the caller.

'But God would, and will. Even murderers can be restored and given a fresh start,' rumbled Roman, 'but only if they repent, and they need to be alive to do that.'

'You still haven't said anything about victims.'

'That's the third principle: compassion. Every judicial execution triggers off more murders in the community. Statistics from around the world show the same thing: societies with the death penalty have higher murder rates than those without. A study in New York showed that the murder rate went up immediately following every execution. The reason is simple: there are some people out there who are not completely balanced, who are hovering on the brink, and news of an execution is enough to tip them over the edge and into murder. Psychologists call it the "copy cat" effect. Every time you execute someone you will trigger off more murders and create new victims. Not very compassionate, eh George?'

During this long explanation Roman had closed the phone fader so the caller could not interrupt. Now he re-opened the fader, but instead of the caller's voice a long beep came down the phone line.

'Sounds as though George has hung up,' said Roman. 'I guess he found the truth a bit more complicated than just killing people.'

Three more open-line calls and two more commercial breaks took Roman to within one minute of midnight, at which point he signed off his show as he always did, by leaning in close to the mike and rumbling to his listeners 'Good night—and God bless', and faded up his famous theme music to fill to the top of the clock.

As the theme ended and the midnight news began, Roman pushed his chair back from the studio desk and heaved a deep and very audible sigh. Another show done, he thought, as he started to scrape together all the bits and pieces of paper that somehow accumulated in the course of a three hour radio talk-back show.

He was crumpling up dated items and throwing them in the bin, and stuffing reusable items into a manilla folder when Andrew Gardner bounded in through the studio door.

Andrew worked for Roman as his producer—sorting out the open line calls, suggesting topics, and lining up the occasional studio guest. He was young, perhaps twenty or twenty-one, ginger-haired, and overflowing with energy and enthusiasm, still excited about working in the radio industry, and with none other than the famous Mark Roman.

'Another great show, Mark,' he burbled.

'Thanks, Andrew,' said Roman. 'Did you have many calls from crackpots to fend off tonight?'

'Only a couple of drunks. I just ask them to wait a minute—then put them on hold for an hour or two.'

'There, I think I've got everything,' said Roman looking around the studio.

'Actually there's a woman on the phone now,' said Andrew, 'who wants to talk to you off air. She may be a crackpot, I don't know. It's that Liz woman you spoke to about half past eleven. You know, the one with the grown-up adopted son. I haven't promised anything, I just said I'd try to find you. I can go back and say you've already left, if you like.'

'But . . . ? If you haven't got rid of her already that means you think I should talk to her, doesn't it?'

'Well . . . she sounds pretty distressed, and I thought you might be able to help her, that's all.'

'All right. Put the call through to the lobby, I'll take it there.'

'You're a top bloke, Mark,' said Andrew as he spun around and hurried back to the switchboard.

Why do I say yes to these things? Roman asked himself, as he stuffed the bulging manilla folder into his untidy briefcase.

Out in the corridor Roman ran into panel operator

19

Peter Stanley packing away the night's commercials.

Peter was another young man, in his early twenties at the latest. Unlike the slim, energetic Andrew, Peter was fat and slow with a round, pudding face that never revealed any expression. But, beneath that unlikely exterior, Roman had found a talented sound-mixer lurking, with surprisingly fast reflexes and a true creative streak.

'Goodnight, Peter.'

'Night, Mr Roman,' replied the young man.

There were only two rooms in the radio station that contained comfortable armchairs—the manager's office and the lobby. Roman sank into one of the chairs in the lobby, the one beside the coffee table that held the telephone. The phone was ringing, but Roman ignored its insistent demand for a moment while he closed his eyes and reminded himself that he couldn't relax just yet.

'Hello, Mark Roman speaking,' he said, picking up the receiver.

'Oh, thank you for taking my call, Mark.' It was the breathy, quavering voice he had spoken to earlier in the evening. 'It's Liz here. I talked to you tonight about my stepson Simon. Do you remember?'

'Yes, I remember, Liz. What can I do for you?'

'There were some things I couldn't tell you on the radio. Or, at least, that I thought I shouldn't tell you. Not in public, that is.'

'Yes?'

'But I'm really worried Mark, really, really worried,' she said, with a sob creeping into her voice.

'About Simon?'

'Yes. We're going to lose him, Mark, I just know we are. If his father can get his claws into him, he'll turn against me. Simon doesn't know what he's really like. He can be very plausible.'

'But if Simon re-establishes contact with his father, does that matter?'

'That's what I didn't want to tell you on the radio. You see my sister, Simon's mother, was murdered. By him.'

'By Simon's father?'

'Yes, that's right. So you can understand why we're so frightened of him.'

'And he's in Australia now is he?'

'I don't know if he has arrived yet, but I know that he's coming.'

'How do you know? And how do you know he is trying to win over Simon?'

'Oh, it's so complicated. That's why I'm ringing you now: to ask you to come and see me and my husband. Let us explain the whole situation. And then you might be able to help.'

'How could I possibly help?'

'By talking to Simon. He's a big fan of yours. He listens to your show most nights. He won't listen to Bertram and me, but if the advice came from you...well...I'm sure he'd listen then.'

'Look, Liz, I don't know that I should get involved in a family matter.'

'Please, Mark. I've listened to you for so long I feel that you're a friend. And we can't think of anyone else to turn to. Just agree to come and see us, Bertram and me. Let us tell you about it. And you can decide then if you want to talk to Simon for us or not.'

Roman knew that he should say no, and say it firmly and at once. But he hesitated. Why, he asked himself, why am I even considering this? He tried to step back and look at his motives for a moment. Was he feeling sympathy for this clearly very distressed woman? Did he simply want to help? There was a little of that, yes, but there was more—curiosity. Roman was honest enough to admit that nothing interested him more than other people's lives. He knew himself to be incurably intrigued by what people did to each other and to themselves.

'Please, Mark, please,' she persisted.

'Well. . . perhaps. . .'

'Oh, thank you! That would be wonderful!'

'When. . .?'

'While Simon's at work would be best. Bertram and I are here all day. He's retired, you know.'

'In the morning then?'

'Yes, yes.'

'Say tomorrow morning at half past ten: how would that be?'

'That would be just wonderful. We'll see you then.'

'Where are you?'

'In Wollstonecraft,' and she gave him an address that he scribbled down on a scrap of paper.

Roman put the phone down with a sinking feeling in his stomach. He had said yes out of curiosity. Now he was deeply wishing he had said no.

Pushing himself wearily to his feet Roman said goodnight to Andrew who responded with a question: 'What did she want?'

'Just some advice,' said Roman, feeling too embarrassed by his ready 'yes' to admit that he was going to visit Liz and her husband in their home.

Roman caught the lift to the basement, flopped into his ageing, dark green Volvo and gunned the engine. As he drove out of the driveway, and out of the radio station's air conditioning, the hot, humid night air swept in through the open driver's window.

It was December, still early summer, but the

22

weather was more like late January or early February, with Sydney going through a burst of sub-tropical weather. The air was very warm, even at a quarter past twelve in the morning, and very still. The humidity gave it a close, pre-breathed quality.

Roman wound up the window, turned on the air conditioning, and headed along the Pacific Highway towards Kirribilli. Night after night, indeed year after year, Roman never ceased to be amazed at the number of cars on the Sydney streets in the early hours of the morning.

He lived in an apartment in an old block of what would once have been called flats. But, when a developer had gutted them and modernised them ten years earlier, they had changed from flats to apartments.

Parking was a problem at night since the old building contained no garages and all the residents parked on the street. The patrons of the Ensemble Theatre, several hundred metres further down McDougall Street, were Roman's allies on the parking front—although they could not have known it. They managed to fill up a good deal of street parking, and their departure after the evening performance left a number of car-sized gaps under the trees beside Milson Park.

On this particular night Roman found one of those gaps, parked the Volvo, and, with his battered brief case under his arm, hurried to his apartment.

He unlocked the door and turned on the lights. The warm, yellow glow was caught and reflected by the darkly varnished timber he favoured in furniture, and Roman felt at home. His first action, after locking the door behind him, was to turn on the television set. Like many people who lived alone, he needed the sound of voices on radio or television to keep him company.

The NBC 'Today Show' was on—a show which left the United States by satellite while Americans were eating breakfast and arrived in Sydney around midnight.

Roman slid open the front windows of the apartment, and a faint clammy breath of tropical air drifted in. Then he set about making himself a Greek salad while keeping one eye and one ear on Bryant Gumble chatting to some Middle East expert or Willard Scott burbling on about the weather in Wisconsin.

Roman ate his salad off a tray on his lap. Every so often his eyes would drift from the TV set to the framed photo on the window sill, the photo that showed Linda nursing young Sharon. It was at mealtimes that he still missed them. At mealtimes he wanted company and conversation.

It was now two years, in fact two years and one month, since the car accident. And he still felt that strange hollowness in his chest when he glanced at the photo.

Roman washed down the salad with a glass of port and then packed his dirty dishes into the dishwasher. In his bedroom he turned on the ceiling fan and opened the window. The slowly revolving fan drew a sluggish breath of hot clammy air into the room, while he stripped off his clothes and washed away the sweat and grime under a cold shower.

Having towelled himself dry, Roman re-closed the bedroom window—if he didn't the morning street noises would wake him. He hunted through his small bookcase full of golfing books, selected *Follow Through* by Herbert W. Wind, and, completely naked, lay down on the bed to read himself to sleep.

The night was hot, the air was sauna hot, even the mattress was hot under his body, and he found it hard to concentrate on the book. His mind kept going back to Liz and her husband—what was his name? Bertram?—and their stepson Simon.

Why had he allowed himself to become involved? He asked the question for the twentieth time. But he really knew the answer: more than anything else he needed to understand. He felt driven to try to understand what made the people he encountered 'tick'.

Eventually Roman's weariness defeated the heat and discomfort, he turned off the light and fell into a restless sleep.

Chapter 2

Roman woke up thinking about murder.

What was it that woman had said to him on the phone? That Simon's mother had been murdered by her South American husband?

Somehow her accusation seemed more shocking to Roman's mind in the cold light of morning—except that it was not cold light but another hot, steamy day when Roman awoke at nine am.

He had managed almost seven hours sleep and he woke to the realisation that—gently revolving ceiling fan not withstanding—seven hours was all the heat was going to allow him to get.

As he showered, shaved and dressed, Roman's mind kept returning to murder. Was Liz right? Had Simon's father been convicted of murder? And had he served a prison sentence? And if so, would he be allowed into Australia? Surely, there would be some law to prevent convicted murders from entering the country?

He re-filled the percolator in his kitchen with freshly ground coffee and water and turned it on. Then, wearing his panama hat as protection against the fierce sun, he left the apartment, locking the door behind him.

From the back of Roman's block of apartments it was possible to climb a flight of stairs to Winslow Lane, behind Our Lady Star of the Sea Catholic church, and zig-zag through several narrow streets to Kirribilli shopping centre. This Roman did every morning without fail.

At the small row of shops that stood in the shadow of the mighty concrete pylons of the Harbour Bridge Roman bought some fresh bread rolls and his morning newspaper. He always bought the *Daily Telegraph Mirror* and was sensitive to the fact that a number of the journalists at the radio station thought it odd that he only ever read a tabloid paper. They, of course, devoured the serious broadsheet newspapers, and looked down their noses at Roman, the ex-disc jockey, who actually *liked* reading the tabloids!

When Roman returned he found his apartment filled with the delicious smell of fresh coffee. With the newspaper spread out on the kitchen table he consumed his usual breakfast of bread rolls and coffee.

Having finished breakfast, read the newspaper, and done ten minutes housekeeping, Roman found it was still too early to set off for Wollstonecraft and the mysterious Liz. If the weather had been milder he would have gone for a walk under the palm trees of Milson Park, but in the heavy, humid air this seemed unattractive.

So, instead, he took up his putter, and with a tumbler at one end of the carpet as his target, did half an hour's putting practice. As he putted he thought again about murder. Had it been one of those violent domestic quarrels that can tragically explode into

27

physical violence? Had this unknown—and unnamed—South American been violent over a long period before the murder? Was he really a dangerous man for Simon to meet?

When his wrist-watch indicated that the inevitable could be put off no longer Roman locked up and went out into McDougall Street where his car was parked. The ageing, dark green Volvo with its 'Resident: Zone 2' sticker on the windscreen, the sticker that gave Roman access to long-duration street parking in Kirribilli, was unmistakable. As he did up the seatbelt and started the motor he was glad of the car's air conditioning and tinted windows.

Roman drove towards Wollstonecraft slowly and reluctantly. Now that he was facing the meeting he was regretting more deeply than ever his agreement to become involved in the private life of a listener. Well, he told himself, it's too late now. The commitment was made and it had to be kept.

The address he was looking for was in Shirley Road, down the far end of the street. It turned out to be an old house by Australian standards: a dark brick, pseudo-Victorian exercise in ugliness. There were bay windows with small leadlight panes, weathered shingles, and creeper growing over the walls. A high brick fence had been built to shield the house from the street, and this was penetrated by two gateways, one at either end of a U-shaped drive. The driveway was cement, and around it the grass had been replaced by gravel and some unhealthy, straggly-looking bushes. There were weeds growing in the gravel and in the cracks in the drive, and the whole house had a slightly dilapidated, uncared-for appearance.

Roman parked in the drive and rang the front door bell. In the quiet suburban surroundings he could hear the faint echo of the bell deep within the house. A long, hot, sweltering time passed. He was about to ring again, when there was a shuffling noise, a click of several locks being unfastened, and the door swung open.

The woman in the doorway might have been in anything from the mid-fifties to the mid-sixties. Her lined and anxious face made it hard to guess her age.

'Mr Roman?' she said in a voice that, to Roman's ear, had the same faint, emotional quaver to it that he had detected on the telephone.

'Yes, that's right. You're Liz I take it? Good morning, I hope I'm on time?'

'Oh, yes I recognise the famous voice,' fluttered Liz. 'Good morning, Mr Roman. Come in, come in.'

She stepped back and Roman entered a dark hallway that was delightfully cool, a welcome escape from the relentless heat outside.

'It's nice and cool in here. And by the way, you must call me Mark, not Mr Roman.'

'Yes, I called you that when I rang up, didn't I?' said Liz. 'That's because I feel I know you, I've listened for so long. But when I saw you on the front step I wasn't sure it would be polite to call you Mark.'

'I insist.'

As they were speaking Liz led Roman down the hall and into a sitting room panelled in dark timber and overly furnished with heavy, old-fashioned furniture. This room was as dark as the hallway and just as pleasantly cool.

'It's the double-brick walls and wide eaves,' explained Liz, 'that keep this house so cool—even on the hottest days.'

'Have you lived here long?'

'Oh, this was our family's Sydney home even before

29

I was born. Take a seat, Mark, and I'll make a pot of tea.'

A cloud of dust puffed out of the over-stuffed sofa as Roman sat down. As Liz walked out of the room, Roman tried to make himself comfortable by removing some of the, seemingly, dozens of small decorative pillows that clustered around him, behind his back and under his elbows.

Left alone he looked around the room, trying to identify the strange sense of deadness the house communicated. The mantelpiece, and all the window-sills, were cluttered with undusted china ornaments and framed photographs. Many of these were old black and white photos of two young girls—on the beach, beside two ponies, nursing a large dog, on a sunlit verandah, and dressed up in school uniforms. To Roman's eye these pictures all belonged to the 1940s.

There was one exception to this pictorial pattern: a large, sepia portrait from an earlier period. It showed a large, stern-faced man wearing a black suit and a heavy black moustache. Cowering beside him was a small, frail looking woman dressed in 1920s-style finery.

Roman was still examining the portrait when Liz returned.

'That's mother and father,' she explained as she set an ornate and ancient silver tray down on a coffee table, 'photographed shortly before their marriage.'

Roman turned around and discovered that a man had entered the room along with Liz, so quietly and so inconspicuously that Roman was taken by surprise to find him there. He had pale grey, wispy hair, a face as featureless as a table-cloth, a faded checked shirt, baggy grey trousers, and slippers on his feet.

'Mark, this is my husband, Bertram.'

Roman reached out and shook the offered hand, receiving in exchange a handshake as lifeless as old rags.

All three of them sat down and Liz began pouring tea into china that had once been very expensive, but was now old and chipped.

'You may smoke if you wish,' she said indicating a heavy glass ashtray on a bookshelf under the window.

'No thanks. I don't smoke.'

'Neither do Bertram and I. We used to, but we both stopped ten years ago. Filthy habit.'

Roman glanced at Bertram who appeared to be too comatose to even nod in agreement.

'Let me start by telling you about Simon's father,' said Liz as she handed around the cups of tea. 'His name is Raffael Escobar. Have you heard of him?'

'No, I don't think so. Should I have?' asked Roman.

'He's a South American as I said, from Ecuador, and he runs a company which exports designer furniture around the world. That's why I thought you might have heard of him.'

'Would I have heard of the company?'

'It's called Earthfast Furniture.'

'Simon's father is the man who runs Earthfast?'

'He not only runs it, Mark, he owns it.'

'I'm impressed. He must be a very rich man, this...what's his name?'

'Raffael Escobar. Yes, Mark, he is very rich. And for the seventeen years we have been raising Simon he has refused to contribute a single dollar to support his own son.'

'I see.'

'He's a disgusting man. It makes me sick just to

31

think about him,' added Liz with a sudden vehemence that surprised Roman.

'And this is the man who murdered your sister, Simon's mother?'

'Yes, he did that. Her name was Peggy; she was a few years younger than me.'

Roman glanced around the room at the clutter of old photographs.

'Yes, that's us,' said Liz following his glance. 'Father was a grazier, and so were grandfather and great-grandfather before him. Peggy and I grew up on the family sheep station in the Dubbo district. Well, there for part of the time, and here in this house for part of the time.'

She took a sip of her tea and then continued.

'Raffael Escobar came to Australia with a polo team in 1961. He was a handsome young man, and rich even then as the heir to the Escobar family fortune, and he swept poor Peggy off her feet. They were married a year later. That's when we lost Peggy, not when she died but when he carried her off to live with him in Ecuador.'

'You lost contact with her did you?'

'She changed. He changed her. She wasn't the same Peggy I grew up with. And anyway, soon after Peggy married that man, Bertram and I got married. Didn't we dear?'

Liz patted her husband's hand as she asked this question, but she did not appear to expect a response. Roman looked hard for a moment at the pale, rumpled figure of Bertram. Not only was he contributing nothing to the conversation, he appeared to be taking no interest in it. His eyes did not flicker upwards but stared resolutely down at his hands, his concentration given over entirely to sipping his tea and nibbling on a plain biscuit.

'There was very little contact for nearly ten years, just Christmas cards and birthday cards. Then in about 1970 we started writing letters again, and in 1975 Betram and I went to Ecuador to visit them. That man had moved the family home from Quito to Guayaquil by then.'

'To where?'

'Guayaquil. It's a big city on the coast, he'd moved there to start his furniture business. We found Peggy living there in a Spanish-style mansion as big as a palace.'

'How old was Simon at this time?'

'He was six, and his older brother was ten.'

'Brother? I didn't know there was a brother?'

'Yes, he was born a few years after Peggy married that man.'

'And what's his name?'

'He insisted that he be named Salvador. Horrible South American name.'

'The "he" who insisted I take it was Raffael Escobar?'

'That's right. When Simon was born four years later Peggy gave him a much more sensible name.'

'So you finally went to visit your sister and her family in 1975...?'

'Yes, and that's when she died. I can't prove it of course but I am certain the reason that man murdered her was because she was thinking of leaving him and bringing the boys back to Australia to live.'

'How did she die? Was it a domestic argument that became violent?'

'He poisoned her.'

This brought Roman's galloping thoughts to a sudden halt. Murder by poison is a very different thing

33

to murder in the heat of a passionate argument. Poisoning is cold and calculating. More than any other form of murder, thought Roman, poison requires what the lawyers call 'malice aforethought'.

'Was this Raffael Escobar convicted of poisoning Peggy?'

'Of course not! He comes from a powerful, wealthy, aristocratic family. At the time, the governor of the province was one of his cousins. There was never any possibility that he would be charged, let alone convicted.'

'Then, how can you be certain you are right, Liz?' asked Roman, consciously dropping into his softest, most mellow voice—he wanted to challenge her allegation without getting her offside. 'How can you be sure that Peggy died from poisoning and that this Escobar man was the killer?'

'Well for a start there's no doubt about the poisoning. There was an inquest, and the coroner said that Peggy died from nicotine poisoning, administered in her coffee. As for that man's guilt: I am certain of that because of Simon's testimony.'

'But surely Simon was only—what?—six years old at the time?'

'But children notice things you know. They see things. And Simon saw his father adding something to his mother's coffee. He saw that. And he told me about it. With his mother dead there was only his Aunt Liz to turn to, and he came and told me about it.'

'And did you tell the authorities?'

'I told the coroner. I stood up at the inquest and told the coroner. Bertram didn't want me to, he said it would cause a lot of difficulty and embarrassment, but I knew I had to do it.'

'And Raffael Escobar was still not charged with murder?'

'I've explained that. His powerful connections protected him.'

Roman took a sip of his tea while he gathered his thoughts.

'And what happened after the inquest?'

'I brought Simon back to Australia. I told that man it was just for a holiday, so that Simon could see his Australian relatives. I wanted the other boy to come too, that Salvador. He was a horrid child, but he was my sister's child and I wanted him to come. But he wouldn't, so I had to leave him behind and just bring Simon. Then when we got here I wrote to that man and told him Simon was staying in Australia and would never go back to Ecuador.'

'How did he respond?'

'He hired lawyers, didn't he Bertram?'

Bertram looked up, his eyes suddenly wide open, as if surprised to find himself drinking tea in the sitting room.

'He hired a big firm of Sydney lawyers,' continued Liz. 'But Bertram and I hired our own lawyers. We went to court and explained about that man being a murderer, and the judge asked Simon questions for a long time. And of course dear little Simon said that he didn't want to go back to his daddy, but he wanted to live in Australia with his Auntie Liz. And because there were no...I forget...what was it Bertram? Mutual legal agreements? Or was it an extradition treaty? I forget, but it was something. There is some treaty or agreement that Australia has with most countries but has never been signed between Australia and Ecuador, and whatever it was, it made it easier for the judge to award legal custody of Simon to us.'

Liz had been talking quickly, almost feverishly, as she told this story, the emotional vibrato in her voice becoming more pronounced as she continued.

Roman tilted back his head and stared at the ceiling for a moment—it was a moulded plaster ceiling heavily decorated with roses and ribbons—while he absorbed all he had been told.

The long silence, filled only with the distant slow ticking of a long-case clock, was finally broken by Liz asking, 'Would you like a second cup of tea, Mark?'

'Ah, yes, yes please,' replied Roman mechanically, pushing his cup forward.

'And in all the years since then,' rumbled Roman thoughtfully, as Liz poured tea into his cup and added milk and sugar, 'in all the years since then you have raised Simon without any contact or support from his father?'

'We have raised Simon as our own son. That's the only way to put it Mark. We've scrimped and saved and gone without to give him the best of everything. We sent him to the best school we could afford and then to university.'

'Please don't take offence, but old grazing families are usually not short of a dollar or two and usually don't need to economise to put one child through a private school. Isn't that true?'

'I can't speak for other families, but in our case there were some bad investments made. Do you remember the nickel boom of the early sixties? And a company called Poseidon? Poor father lost hundreds of thousands of dollars there. And then the bottom dropped out of the wool market and he had to borrow heavily to keep the property out at Dubbo running. By the time wool prices came good again it was too late for us, our sheep station was gone—a mortgagee

36

sale. All that was left was this house and a few small investments. And that's all that Bertram and I have to live on now.'

Roman leaned back in the sofa and looked at Liz through half closed eyelids. She was not looking at him now, but staring down into her tea cup, her voice becoming fainter as she spoke. Then she swallowed hard and looked up at Roman with what is often called a 'brave face'.

'But we don't complain,' she said loudly and firmly. 'We make the best of things, don't we Bertram? And by cutting corners and being careful and by going without things for ourselves we've been able to give Simon the best.'

'You have no children of your own?'

'Simon is our own. That's how we think of him. But, to answer your question, no there are no others. Bertram and I were never blessed with our own offspring.'

Roman finished his tea and replaced the cup on the handsome old silver tray.

'Which brings us to today,' he said, 'and the problem you called me about.'

'Oh, yes,' said Liz with a gush. 'I'm terribly sorry about taking so much of your time. But I had to explain the background so that you could understand the problem.'

Roman leaned back in the sofa. He was no longer thinking about the story Liz was telling, he was simply absorbing it, and, at the same time, he was absorbing the atmosphere of this house and of this tight little family circle—Liz, Bertram and Simon. Was Bertram always as blank as he was now, or did he once play a more active role in the family?

'At university Simon did a course in computers and

commerce. He always was a very bright boy. He finished his studies at the end of last year. It was earlier this year that Bertram and I went along to see him graduate, looking so very handsome in his cap and gown. We were very proud of him.'

Liz stopped for a moment, apparently lost in silent admiration, or love, for her nephew/stepson.

'You were saying?' prompted Roman.

'Ah, yes. I was saying that at the end of last year there were jobs advertised on the noticeboards at Simon's university, and one of those jobs was just perfect for him. It described exactly the sort of qualifications he was going to graduate with, and it covered exactly the areas he was interested in. Well, Simon got that job—out of hundreds of people who applied. At the time we were delighted, but now I know it was all engineered.'

'Who engineered it?'

'That man!'

'Raffael Escobar?'

'Exactly! Now you can understand what we're up against.'

'I'm afraid I don't, though. I still don't understand.'

'I told you that man still wants to get his son back. After killing his mother and ignoring him all these years he wants to steal him back from us. So he hired his solicitors, or private detectives, or someone, to find out what Simon was doing at university. And then he set up a company specifically to hire Simon. So that Simon would be working for him and could come under his influence.'

'You mean to say that Raffael Escobar owns this company that Simon is working for?'

'Exactly!'

'How do you know?'

38

'I sent Bertram into the Corporate Affairs office to do a company search.'

'I used to be a solicitor's clerk before I retired,' said Bertram.

Roman was startled to hear the grey, wispy man in the corner armchair speak. The voice sounded soft and short of breath, but it had none of the emotional quaver of Liz's voice. So, thought Roman, Bertram was not as detached from reality as he appeared. And despite the unfocused vagueness of his pale, milky eyes he had been following the conversation.

'And what did you find?' asked Roman, turning towards the old man.

'That Network Systems Proprietary Limited is a wholly owned subsidiary of Earthfast Furniture, which, in turn is registered in Ecuador.' Having said his piece Bertram lapsed back into silence, like a snail retreating into its shell.

'But lots of big companies have set up computer divisions,' protested Roman. 'Isn't it assuming too much to imagine that Escobar set up this company purely for the purpose of employing Simon?'

'But he did Mark, he did!' insisted Liz, with a fervent passion. 'Why would he set up the company in Australia if he was not after Simon? And why was the job designed exactly to suit Simon's needs? And why was it advertised just as Simon was finishing his studies?'

A silence settled on the room as Roman absorbed this. He found his mind moving into that sort of half-dreamy state which is the opposite to rational thought; instead of reasoning, he was trying to feel his way to the truth of what seemed to be a strange situation. It was like looking at a painting and trying to recapture what the artist felt when it was being painted.

Finally Roman broke his reverie to ask, 'But why did you go and do that company search in the first place?'

'Because of the letter.'

'What letter?'

'I'm sorry Mark, I'm explaining this badly,' said Liz. 'It's because I'm so upset about it. Simon received a letter from that man. At his work address. Well, of course, Simon brought it home and showed it to us. It was full of lies of course, but what I immediately thought was: how did that man get Simon's work address? And that made me wonder about the company and about how Simon got the job in the first place, so I sent Bertram in to do the company search.'

'I see. If Escobar wanted to contact Simon why not simply write to him here, at this address?'

'If he'd tried that I would have burned the letter at once!' snapped Liz.

'Without letting Simon see it?'

'My life is dedicated to looking after that boy, and protecting him from that evil man.'

'I see. What did the letter say?'

'Lies, just lies. The sort of things you'd expect that man to say.'

'May I see the letter?'

'It's been destroyed. After Simon and Bertram and I had all read it, I said the best thing we could do was burn the letter and Simon agreed.'

'But still, it seems a bit extreme to set up a whole company just so he could write a letter to his son.'

'The letter is just the first step, Mark, I know it is. That man doesn't just want to write to Simon, he wants to control him.'

'Still, if he's prepared to go to such lengths, and such

expense, to restore contact with his son—perhaps he really loves Simon?'

'Love? Love? That man lives off pride and hatred! Nothing he does is motivated by love!'

'But there must be some sort of commitment by Raffael Escobar to Simon. Otherwise, why would he spend the money it must have cost to start this company?'

'You don't understand him, Mark, I do. He is a very wealthy, very proud man. He has lost one of his sons and his pride is hurt. He can easily afford to spend money, in a devious and manipulative way, to get him back into his clutches again.'

'Why doesn't Simon just resign from his job then?'

'Simon is a dear, sweet boy, and rather naive where that man is concerned. Simon refuses to see the danger. I've explained it to him, I've pleaded with him to resign. But he says he likes the work, and with his lack of experience he couldn't get a similar job anywhere else, and he just doesn't see the danger.'

Roman rested his chin on his hand and sighed deeply; this was a messy domestic situation that was really none of his business. He was about to say so when Liz spoke again.

'That's where you can come in, Mark,' she said. 'Simon is a big fan of yours. He'll pay more attention to you than he will to either Bertram or me. Will you talk to him for me?'

'What do you want me to say?'

'Get him to understand how worried I am. Get him to see that the company he works for is owned by a murderer—the murderer of his own mother. Get him to agree to leave the company for his own safety and for my peace of mind.'

'I don't know that I can achieve any of those things, Liz,' explained Roman gently.

'But do try! Please Mark, tell me you'll try! You'll at least speak to Simon for me, will you do that much?'

Roman knew that he should say no, and say it quickly and firmly. But saying no to tearful requests was something he had never been able to do. Roman knew his own weaknesses, and he knew that underneath his solid and impassive face he turned to pure marshmallow when someone pleaded with him emotionally. He recognised that the best he could do would be to agree to the very minimum.

'Won't he think it odd, for me to talk to him about this?' said Roman, 'After all, it is a family matter.'

'Tell him you've spoken to me,' said Liz. 'Tell him bluntly that I've asked you to talk to him. He used to confide in me when he was little, but as boys grow up they confide less and less. You know how it is.'

'Well, I suppose I can talk to him.'

'Oh, thank you Mark, thank you!'

'But you've got to understand that it is most unlikely that I can make any difference. It's not my job to tell people where they should work. Really, in the end all I can do is sit down and listen to him. Perhaps if he talks openly to me that will help him sort it out for himself. But I won't tell him what to do.'

'I'm so pleased that you've agreed to help, Mark,' gushed Liz, who appeared not to have heard his carefully qualified remarks.

Roman asked for Simon's telephone number and Liz handed him a business card that had been sitting on the silver tray the whole time. So, thought Roman, she was certain that I would agree to what she asked.

Roman held the small card in his thick, stubby fingers and read its printed message: Simon Miller,

Systems Analyst, Network Systems Pty Ltd. The address and phone number were in Crows Nest.

He slipped the card into his top pocket then made his farewells. There was another limp handshake from Bertram and a lot of gushing from Liz.

Outside the heat hit him like a blast from a furnace, and, as he walked back to his car through the blazing, brilliant sunlight, he found his thoughts wandering. The visit he had just made into a tight and intense little family circle had left him dazed and disoriented.

The Volvo was like an oven and the windows had to be wound down to flush out the over-heated air, then wound back up again before he turned on the air-conditioning.

At the Pacific Highway he turned left and headed towards Crows Nest. He had no intention of calling on Simon Miller unannounced, but since the suburb was so close he might as well take a look at the address.

Roman parked his car in the Crows Nest shopping centre, and went for a slow walk checking out street numbers. When he found the building he went inside to take a look at the building directory. Network Systems, he discovered, occupied only one floor of this small office block, which meant, he assumed, that it was quite a small company.

Back on the street he bought a salad roll then hurried back to the air-conditioning of his car to eat it as he drove home to Kirribilli.

As he drove, he picked up his car phone and dialled Simon's number. But, as the phone started to ring at the other end, he got cold feet and hung up hurriedly. He decided he should think through his approach carefully before making contact.

Back in his apartment, Roman turned to his usual

after lunch entertainment: the crosswords in that morning's *Telegraph-Mirror*. But, even with three crossword puzzles to move between and his *Chamber's 20th Century Dictionary* at his elbow, Roman could neither concentrate on, nor enjoy, what he was doing.

He knew what the problem was: he was putting off making that appointment to see Simon Miller, and the longer he put it off, the harder it would be. At length, he pulled the business card out of his pocket, grabbed the telephone, and dialled again.

'Good afternoon, Network Systems. Can I help you?'

'May I speak to Simon Miller please?'

'Hold the line, please.'

There were several clicks and buzzes and then another phone started ringing. Roman had still not planned what he was going to say when the phone was answered. As he did so often on the air, he was leaving it to his instinct to give him the right words.

'Miller speaking, can I help you?'

'Mr Miller, my name is Mark Roman.'

There was a longish pause at the other end, and then the words, 'You mean—from the radio?'

'Yes, that's me.'

'It's a pleasure to speak to you, Mr Roman, I often listen to your show. Do you have a computer problem?'

'I'm afraid not. The fact is that your Aunt Liz has been talking to me.'

'At some length no doubt,' said Miller with a laugh.

'At considerable length,' said Roman, rumbling out his most persuasive radio voice, 'and she has told me how worried she is about...well, about you...and about your father.'

'Ah, now I understand. This is part of Liz's campaign to make me resign.'

44

'All I have promised to do is to talk to you. Or, better still, to listen to you.'

'It's all right, Mr Roman, I understand. I'm sure you had no option but to agree. Over the past seventeen years I have learned that the only way to stop Aunt Liz talking your ears off is to agree with her. It's what I usually do. So I'm quite happy to get together and have a chat with you. As long as I'm allowed to ask you some questions about you and radio.'

'Agreed,' said Roman hurriedly. 'Suggest a place and time.'

'Well, if you feel like popping up to Crows Nest we could have a cup of coffee this afternoon.'

Chapter 3

It was shortly after three o'clock when Roman found the small Crows Nest coffee shop where Simon Miller had suggested they meet. Roman's only requirement had been that the meeting place must be air-conditioned.

Roman was a few minutes early, so he ordered a cappuccino and waited.

After five minutes a young man in his early twenties walked in off the street. He had curly black hair and a round face which did not look as though it was in the habit of smiling a lot.

The young man approached Roman's table.

'Mr Roman?' he asked.

'You recognised me?'

'I've seen your picture in the paper from time to time. I'm Simon Miller—pleased to meet you.'

They shook hands and the young man sat down.

'Thanks for agreeing to see me,' said Roman.

'A pleasure. As I say, I've been a listener of yours for years, so I'm happy to take the opportunity to meet you.' Simon ordered a coffee from a passing waitress and then asked, 'Now, what's all this about?'

'It's a bit awkward, to be honest,' said Roman uncomfortably. 'All your Aunt's idea you understand.'

'No need to apologise. As I said on the phone, when Aunt Liz wants you to do something you usually end up doing it.'

'In this case, she wants me to talk to you about your father.'

'Ah, yes. Raffael Escobar.'

'Do you have any memories of him at all?'

'I remember absolutely nothing. My earliest memories go back to when I was about seven. And that was nearly a year after I moved to Australia.'

'Isn't that unusual? Having no infant memories at all, I mean. Most people can remember one or two things from their infancy.'

'It probably is unusual. I think there is some sort of mental block there, a kind of amnesia, shutting of traumatic memories. After all, my mother was murdered, and apparently I was able to give evidence that my father was guilty. That would have to be about maximum trauma for a small child.'

'I imagine so. So you have grown up in Australia quite happily? With no sense of loss?'

'None at all. Aunt Liz and Uncle Bertram have been very good to me. And I enjoyed my school years—I did quite well academically—so I'm not aware of any sense of loss.'

'Did you never wonder, as a child, what your father was like? Or your brother?'

'Or my dead mother? Yes, I did wonder sometimes. The normal curiosity of a child I guess. When I asked Aunt Liz about my mother she told me all about their childhood together as sisters. And there are those photographs of mother when she was young all around the house. So I always felt I knew her a bit, in a way.'

'And your father?'

'Aunt Liz wouldn't talk about him. I knew his name, of course. And when Earthfast furniture began being imported into this country I read a bit about him in the newspapers. Now I think about it, there must have been some curiosity there because I always read those stories avidly. Mind you, they never told me much, they were just business stories.'

'And there's an older brother isn't there?'

'Yes. I've been told his name is Salvador. And that's all I know about him.'

'Was there never any contact with your father when you were growing up?'

'Never. Aunt Liz sometimes complained about the fact that he was a wealthy man who never sent any money to support his youngest son.'

'Did that ever bother you?'

'Not especially. I had my family in Aunt Liz and Uncle Bertram. If I was missing out on something it was something I don't remember having. And it's hard to truly miss what you don't remember.'

Roman ordered another coffee from the waitress who was leaning indolently against the cappuccino machine. While it was coming they made small talk.

'Do you enjoy doing talk-back?' asked Simon.

'Yes,' said Roman firmly, 'I enjoy conversation. I'm interested in people, and in what makes them tick. And that's why I find radio talk-back so stimulating to do.'

'You've got a panic button that you can push if someone swears, haven't you?'

'That's right. The whole show runs through a seven-seconds delay, so if someone says the wrong thing

I can cut it off seven seconds before it gets to air.'

'Do you have to do that often?'

'Very rarely. And almost never for swearing. Defamation is a much bigger worry. If, for instance, someone rings up to complain about the lack of service at certain chain stores, or at a chain of fast food outlets. As long as they mention no names I can listen to their complaint and make some suggestions about how they can handle it. But if, after making some pretty strong complaints, they then name the place, well, that's defamatory and I have to hit the button and cut them off before the name goes to air.'

'How often would that happen?'

'Maybe once a month. Listeners who ring up to complain are told not to name names, and they only forget that rule if they get carried away.'

'So you've got someone who sorts out your incoming calls for you?'

'Yes. Andrew talks to each caller for long enough to find out what topic they want to discuss, and whether or not they are good talent—whether they are articulate and interesting and so on.'

'So how does your producer communicate with you?'

'Through a computer link. He types information about each caller onto a computer screen, and I have a slave screen that shows the same information in my studio.'

'And which of you decides which call to take next?'

'I insist that Andrew does that. Only Andrew has spoken to the caller, and only Andrew knows who is good talent and who is not. So he has to make a production decision about who goes next. He has to balance up different topics, and points of view, and types of callers, to give me a program with variety, with light and shade.'

'I didn't realise there was so much to it,' said Simon as Roman's second cup of coffee was served.

'Now,' said Roman, 'let's get back to your father. You knew about him, but there was no contact for seventeen years?'

'That about sums it up.'

'And now you are working for him?'

'It's quite a coincidence, isn't it?'

'Your Aunt Liz doesn't seem to think it's a coincidence!'

'Just quietly, Mr Roman, Aunt Liz is quite big on conspiracy theories. Give her one and a half facts and she'll turn it into a conspiracy.'

'Well, she did suggest to me that your father engineered the whole arrangement.'

'I don't believe that.'

'He just *happened* to set up his computer software company in Australia?'

'Australia has a good reputation in the software field. And it's probably cheaper to set up here than in, say, the United States.'

'But then, so I'm told, a letter arrived from him. How do you explain that?'

'He must have discovered my name on a staff list. Or someone pointed it out to him. Either way he took advantage of the coincidence of my working for him to write me a letter.'

'When did this letter arrive?'

'About three months ago.'

'Really? I had the impression from Liz it was quite recently.'

'That's because Aunt Liz has been brooding about it. And the longer she broods, the worse it gets.'

'What was the letter like?'

'Quite friendly. I thought it was a very pleasant letter, all things considered.'

'What did it say?'

'The main point was that he was asking me to write to him. Just to re-establish contact after all these years, you understand. He said he still loved my mother, and still grieved for her, and, naturally he denied having anything to do with her death.'

'And that's all?'

'It wasn't a very long letter.'

'I gather it's been destroyed.'

'Yes. Aunt Liz insisted.'

'And did you respond to his suggestion? Did you write him a letter?'

'Oh no! Of course not!'

'Why not?'

'It would have upset Aunt Liz too much. I couldn't do that. Not after all she's done for me.'

'If it wasn't for Liz, would you have written back?'

This question seemed to surprise Simon, and there was a long and thoughtful silence before he replied, 'I don't know. I might have.'

Roman finished the last of his second cup of coffee, put the cup down on the table top, and said, 'What Liz has asked me to do is to talk you into resigning from Network Systems.'

'Well. . . in that case. . .'

'Don't worry,' interrupted Roman, 'I have no intention of even trying to do that. That's what she asked me to do, as I say, but all I promised was to talk to you. And I've done that.'

'And it's been a pleasure meeting you, Mr Roman, having been a listener for so many years, but I should get back to the office now.'

'Just one question before you go, Simon.'

'Yes?'

'What made Liz contact me *now*—I mean three months after the letter from your father came?'

'It's just that she's been brooding on it, as I said, and has finally worked up a head of steam. Although it might have been triggered off by the arrival of this man from head office.'

'What man?'

'Aunt Liz didn't tell you about him?'

'No, she didn't. You tell me.'

'Well, there's a chap from Earthfast head office, Ecuador, who's just arrived in Australia on a flying visit—to check over how the software development is coming on I suppose.'

'When did he arrive?'

'It's all been fairly sudden. We heard he was coming only on Monday. He arrived yesterday and was in the office for an hour or so. Mind you, I didn't even get a chance to speak to him yesterday. I still haven't been introduced to him. He spent most of yesterday getting over jet lag, and this morning in the boardroom with the manager and the accountant.'

'I see. This man is an Ecuadorian—or whatever the proper word is?'

'Yes, he is.'

'Then Liz might be afraid that he is an emissary from your father, mightn't she?'

'Yes. . .I suppose so.'

'Did you tell her about this man?'

'Yes, I told her when I got home from work yesterday.'

'That might have triggered off her call to me last night.'

'I guess so.'

'But you haven't spoken to this visitor yet?'

52

'I haven't been introduced, but we did speak briefly. On his way out to lunch he stopped at my desk and asked if we might have a private meeting this afternoon after work.'

'Did you agree?'

'Yes, of course. They pay my salary, so it's good policy to be agreeable. We are going to sit down over a cup of coffee at half past five.'

'Does Liz know yet?'

'No, this only happened today.'

'What will you do if this man is indeed a representative of your father? What will you say if he asks you to write to Raffael Escobar, or even visit him in Ecuador?'

Simon laughed with all the relaxed confidence of youth. 'I'll be diplomatic,' he said. 'I'll agree to what I have to in order to keep my job, and no more.'

After Simon Miller had gone back to his office Roman sat in the air-conditioned comfort of the coffee shop for some time, his chin on his hand, lost in thought.

Perhaps, thought Roman, Liz was right after all. Perhaps Simon was being a bit young and naive, while Raffael Escobar was manoeuvring very carefully. Since Escobar knew where Simon was (the letter proved that) surely anyone he sent to check on the operations of Network Systems would come in a personal as well as a business capacity?

Roman stepped out of the coffee shop into the heat and continuous piercing roar of traffic on the Pacific Highway with these thoughts whirling around in his head.

At Kirribilli he found the parking spot opposite his apartment occupied. In the end he had to park two blocks away and trudge back through the still, humid air.

After stripping off his clothes and standing under a cold shower for ten minutes, he started to feel more like a human being and less like a lobster in the last stages of boiling.

I've done what I can, thought Roman. I've done all that I promised Liz I would.

But, somehow this self-excusing was unsatisfactory. If Raffael Escobar was really trying to manoeuvre Simon into a renewed contact then Roman knew that he had done nothing to prevent this. But worse than that, he felt that he still did not understand this jigsaw puzzle of people and emotions.

Roman picked up the telephone and re-dialled Simon Miller's office number, but this time, when the receptionist answered he said, 'It's Mark Roman calling. I believe you have a visitor in the office, a gentleman from Ecuador, from head office: may I speak to him please?'

There was a pause, then the receptionist said, 'Hold the line, please.'

During the long silence that followed Roman wondered if he was doing the right thing.

Eventually there was a click, a ring, a telephone was picked up, and a heavily accented voice said: 'Good afternoon, can I help you?'

'I'm a friend of Simon Miller,' said Roman, stretching the truth a little, 'and of his Aunt and Uncle. I wonder if I could meet with you, and have a chat.'

There was another pause, not a long one this time, and then the voice said, 'Yes, if you wish.'

'What time would suit you?'

'Well, I have an appointment at five-thirty and I'm not sure how long that meeting will be. How would seven o'clock suit you?'

'Fine. I'll see you at seven. In the office of Network Systems?'

'Yes, that would be best.'

'I'll see you there then, at seven o'clock.'

Roman hung up and immediately lifted the phone again and dialled the home number of his producer.

'Andrew? Mark here, sorry to disturb you at home. I'm going to be a bit late tonight. I have to see a man at Crows Nest at seven o'clock. I'm not sure how long that meeting will last but at the very latest I should be at the station by eight thirty. So, can you get the studio set up for me and all the routine things done? Thanks. Oh, and don't forget to check the wires to see if there are any stories we can use. Okay. See you tonight.'

For Roman arriving at eight thirty for a show that began at nine was cutting things a little too fine, but he was hoping the meeting would be a short one and he would not be quite that late.

He spent the next hour doing his routine preparation: clipping news items out of the *Telegraph-Mirror* that might make suitable talk-back topics. Each item was pasted onto a sheet of foolscap paper, and underneath Roman jotted down some notes for comments he might like to make or questions he might put to the listeners.

Feeling he had done enough work for the time being Roman hunted through his CD collection and found some music he felt like listening to: *Hits of the 60s*. It took him back to his days as a disc jockey. He stripped off his shirt, splashed cold water on his face, turned on the ceiling fan, lay down on the sofa and half dozed while the music played.

At six o'clock he drove up the Pacific Highway to

Crows Nest again. Propping the Volvo in the council car park in Alexander Street he walked half a block to Eric's Seafood Cafe. It was the kind of old fashioned cafe that delighted Roman—lino-topped tables and plain but deliciously fresh seafood. He had an entrée of calimari followed by lemon sole and washed down with Perrier.

Forty-five minutes later Roman retrieved his car and drove the four blocks further up the highway that took him to the office block he was looking for. As he drove he noticed that the weather was changing in some subtle way. The heat was still oppressive and the stillness uncanny but the blazing sun was now invisible behind a bank of clouds and the air seemed to tremble with the quiet expectancy that precedes a storm.

It took a frustrating ten minutes to find a parking spot, and as Roman locked the car and hurried towards the offices of Network Systems he was worried about being late for the appointment.

The computer company occupied the third floor of a wide, stumpy looking glass fronted office block. The entrance lobby was all sliding glass doors, paving tiles and potted palms. Roman felt a hollow sense of apprehension in his stomach as the automatic lift quietly hummed him up to the third floor. His curiosity was driving him towards an interview that he knew was going to be an uncomfortable one.

He stepped out of the lift to find himself facing a reception desk. It was unoccupied. Indeed, all of the desks in the large, open plan office behind the reception desk were unoccupied. All the lights were turned off, and, while there was ample sunlight spilling in through the tinted office windows, the effect was one of eerie dimness. And silence.

Roman's feet made no sound as he walked forward

over the soft, deep-pile carpet. 'Hello?' he called as he advanced. 'Is anyone there?'

He stood and listened. Silence. No sound of a keyboard clicking in the distance, no phones, nothing.

'Is anyone about?'

There was no response.

Roman walked forward through the strange half-twilight between the deserted desks, each covered with half completed work. It was like walking the decks of the *Marie Celeste*.

'Hello?'

As his voice came echoing back through the silence Roman realized that he didn't even know the name of the man he was going to see. He was annoyed with himself for not asking when he rang for the appointment.

At one end of the football-field-sized office the open plan ended and there were a number of enclosed offices. Roman decided that would be 'mahogany row', the executive area. He turned in that direction.

'Is there anyone there?' he called again.

There were not even any cleaners in the building, the silence was complete.

Roman arrived at the cluster of enclosed offices. The first two had glass walls and were as deserted as all the other desks. Beyond them was a timber-panelled wall in which were two doors. Roman tried the first door and found it locked, but the second swung silently open at his touch.

It revealed a large, book-lined office with padded leather armchairs and a sofa. Roman advanced several steps. There was a glass-topped coffee table with several unwashed cups on it.

At the end of the office was a large executive desk—the 'half-an-acre-of-oak' kind—and lying sprawled across it was a man, face down and motionless.

'Excuse me?' said Roman loudly, hoping that this was just a man who had fallen asleep at his desk.

The sprawled figure did not move. Roman hurried forward, reached over and tugged at the sleeve that lay across a leather-edged blotting pad.

'Excuse me,' repeated Roman as he did so. The arm fell back limply onto the desk, and Roman hurried around to the chair side so that he could reach over and feel for a pulse. There was no need.

Once he could see the man's back he could also see the knife protruding from it.

Roman forced himself to reach out and touch the limp hand on the blotter. He could detect no pulse, and was about to pick up the phone to dial triple-0 when he stopped himself. The police might want to check that phone for fingerprints. He walked back into the main office and picked up the phone on the first desk he came to.

He dialled zero for an outside line, then three more zeros.

'Emergency—which service do you want?'

'Police.'

There was a momentary switching delay, then a ringing phone and a voice saying, 'Police'.

'I'd like to report a murder,' said Roman. 'I've just arrived in an office to keep an appointment and I've found a body here. He's been stabbed.'

'Are you certain he's dead?'

'I could find no pulse.'

'Whereabouts are you?'

'At a company called Network Systems,' said Roman and gave the address.

'Can I have your name please sir?'

58

'Roman—Mark Roman.'

'The radio star?'

'Yes.'

'You stay where you are, Mr Roman, and we'll have someone with you in a few minutes.'

Roman dropped the phone back into its cradle and looked around the empty office. Knowing that he was only metres away from a corpse made the silence not only uncanny but sinister.

An abrupt crash of thunder made him jump nervously. Out beyond the tinted glass office walls towards the Blue Mountains a fork of lightning stabbed the sky. Then came the low rumble of distant thunder and another megavolt spark lit up the clouds.

Roman turned back towards the office where he had left the murder victim, his curiosity overcoming his sense of apprehension. He walked in and stood in the middle of the plush pile carpet for a while, staring at the figure slumped across the desk.

Then he walked forward until he almost bumped the desk, crouched down to the level of the desktop and looked closely at the victim's face. Even in death it was a darkly handsome face, with distinctively Latin American features.

Roman straightened up and looked around the room. Hanging on a coat rack behind the door was a jacket from a man's suit. Perhaps, he thought, I can find out who this man is. He crossed the room and began feeling through the jacket pockets. There was a silk dress-handkerchief in the top pocket and, in the side pockets, a hotel roomkey and some small change, but no wallet.

Then in an inside pocket Roman found a passport.

He stared at the small, vinyl folder in his hands, with the coat of arms of Ecuador stamped in gold on the front. Inside was a small colour photograph. It was a smiling photograph and showed a pleasant, open face, the face of the victim. Surrounding it were printed words in Spanish and various visa stamps.

He turned the passport around and then read the name that went with the face—Salvador Escobar. Roman drew a sharp breath. The emissary from head office, the man now lying dead in the corner of the office, was Simon's brother.

Once he had returned the passport to the jacket pocket, Roman's mind began to race. . . Simon had been due to meet this man for a private discussion at half past five. Had that meeting taken place? Had Salvador Escobar revealed his identity to Simon? And if so, how had Simon taken it? Would he have been upset, or would he have taken it calmly? What had they talked about?

Roman paced up and down as he thought. . . Salvador Escobar had mentioned on the phone his appointment at five thirty, but no other appointment. If there was no other appointment then Simon was the last person to see the victim alive. Apart from the murderer, that is. Unless. . .

Roman hurried back out into the main office and picked up the phone he had used to call the police. This time he dialled Liz's number.

'Hello?' The voice at the end of the line belonged to Bertram.

'Hello, Bertram? It's Mark Roman here.'

'Oh? Good evening, Mr Roman. Are you calling for Liz?'

'No, it's Simon I'm after. Is he there?'

'No, not at the moment.'

'Are you expecting him?'

'Oh yes, certainly. Indeed, he is usually home by

this hour. He is as a rule very punctual, young Simon.'

'Did he warn you that he might be late tonight?'

'No. . .no. . .I don't think so. He didn't say anything to me.'

'Can I speak to Liz please? He might have told her.'

'Liz? Ah, yes, well Liz is in the kitchen cooking. I'll see if she can come to the phone.'

There was a loud clunk as the handset at the other end was placed down on a hard surface. Then he could discern the voice of Bertram calling out, 'Liz dear, it's Mr Roman on the phone for you.'

A moment later came the sound of Liz's voice echoing as though down a corridor, 'My hands are covered in flour; take a message; say I'll call back.'

'Did you hear that, Mr Roman?' asked Bertram, returning to the phone.

'Yes I did, thanks. There's no message. Just tell her I'll call again tomorrow.'

'Certainly, Mr Roman. Goodbye.'

As he heard the phone click into disconnect, it occurred to Roman that the dead man was the nephew of Liz and Bertram. Should he have told them that Salvador Escobar was dead? Somehow he felt it was not his place to do that.

Roman replaced the phone with another fact added to the torrent of thoughts in his head: Simon was not at home. And he was missing unexpectedly, without explanation. Again Roman asked himself, What happened at the meeting between Simon and Salvador?

These speculations were interrupted by the electrical whirr of lift doors opening. Two uniformed police officers stepped out, a young man and a young woman.

'Over here officer,' called Roman.

'Would you be Mr Mark Roman?' said the young policeman as he approached.

'Yes I am. And the body is through that doorway in the end office.'

The policewoman went to look, while the male officer stayed with Roman.

'Exactly when did you find the body, sir?' he asked.

'Five past seven it would have been,' said Roman, 'My appointment was for seven o'clock but I was running a bit late.'

The policewoman returned and muttered coldly, 'No signs of life,' then unclipped a small radio from her belt and called in to say that an ambulance would not be needed.

There was an awkward silence. Presumably, thought Roman, these two had no function except to stand guard over the body. And over me? he wondered.

The male officer broke the silence. 'I quite often hear your radio program Mr Roman,' he said. 'Whenever I'm driving home late at night.'

'I'm pleased,' said Roman. It was what he always said in response to that remark. What else could he say?

'I enjoy it,' continued the policeman, in a rather shy and awkward manner. 'It's a good show.'

'Thank you,' muttered Roman. Vague compliments were always difficult to respond to.

The lift hummed again and two men Roman assumed to be plainclothes officers stepped out. These two ignored Roman while they spoke in hushed voices to their uniformed colleagues and took a look at the corpse.

Roman sat on the edge of a desk and waited.

The lift was busy again and, over the next ten minutes, it disgorged a scientific officer carrying a black leather case rather like a photographer's, a smartly dressed woman carrying a doctor's bag, and two heavily built men wearing blue overalls.

Roman turned away from them and stared out of the window.

It was dark outside now and the office lights had been turned on. The first drops of rain began to appear on the glass, each wet bead reflecting the office lights as it dribbled down the pane.

'Mr Roman?'

The voice from over his shoulder made him jump. He turned around and found himself facing the pair of plainclothes officers who arrived ahead of the rest of the crowd.

'I'm Detective Kline this is Detective Fitzpatrick,' said the elder of the two, 'I understand you discovered the body?'

'That's right,' said Roman.

'Tell me about it,' said Kline, and so Roman did.

Chapter 4

Throughout his lengthy interview with Kline and Fitzpatrick Roman kept glancing at his watch. He still had a radio show to do that night. Would the detectives want to keep him here? Or would they let him go and do the show?

'Now, let's go back over this again, Mr Roman,' said Kline in a weary voice. 'You had no idea this man was Salvador Escobar until you found his passport in his wallet?'

'That's right. Simon didn't know his name when he told me of his arrival from Ecuador, and I didn't think to ask when I made the appointment. Look can we continue this later? Much later? Like after midnight?'

'Are my questions annoying you, Mr Roman?'

'Of course not. But I am supposed to be on the air in an hour's time and I'd really like to leave for the studio now.'

'I'm not sure that's going to be possible, Mr Roman. Why don't you ring the radio station and tell them to put someone else on in your place?'

'It's too late to do that, Mr Kline. It's not a disc jockey show, they can't just put anyone on the air. And the station doesn't have very many standby talk-back presenters who can fill in, and none who could do it at such short notice.'

Kline turned to his partner and raised a questioning eyebrow.

'Why don't I go with him, Jim?' responded Fitzpatrick.

And so it was arranged. Roman would take Detective Fitzpatrick with him to the radio station, do his show, then return to answer more questions.

As Roman drove down the Pacific Highway with Fitzpatrick in the front passenger's seat, he asked, 'Why am I getting all this attention? Am I a suspect?'

'I can think of no reason to regard you as a suspect Mr Roman—'

'Mark, please. I'd far rather be called Mark.'

'If you wish. It's just a matter of proper procedure at this early stage of an investigation.'

'And I don't want to go on calling you Detective Fitzpatrick all night: what's your Christian name?'

The policeman hesitated for a moment, and then, as if cornered by the radio star's avuncular manner replied, 'Ian.'

'The other thing I need to know is how much I can say about this on the air. Can I tell my listeners about this, Ian?'

'We'd prefer that you didn't, Mark.'

'Come on. This is a story. It'll be in all the newspapers tomorrow. Since I found the body I'm going to look pretty stupid if I don't break the story tonight.'

'In that case, you'll just have to say as little as you can.'

'So what are the rules?'

'The most important rule is that you don't identify the victim until the next of kin have been notified. And you need to be careful about saying it was definitely murder.'

'But it has to be murder! Unless he was able to reach around and stab himself in the back!'

The detective ignored Roman's sarcasm and said, 'And we'd also prefer that you didn't mention his nationality as yet. As he's the son of a wealthy foreigner, we'll have to tread warily, and we don't want diplomats breathing down our necks on a murder investigation.'

'Ah, so you do admit it's murder then?'

'What it is and what we want to say in public at this stage are two different things.'

As the drive to the radio station continued Fitzpatrick's determination to keep Roman silent on the murder weakened. He and Kline had found the media useful in a number of previous investigations, and he was reluctant to offend such a powerful media figure as Roman.

The Pacific Highway shone like fresh varnish under the streetlights and flashing neons; the rain that had accompanied the electrical storms had stopped, leaving behind wet roads and warm air saturated with moisture, like a bathroom after a long shower.

At the radio station Roman provoked raised eyebrows and puzzled expressions from his producer and panel operator when he introduced Fitzpatrick as 'a plainclothes policeman...a detective'.

'What's this all about, Mark?' asked Andrew Gardner. 'Have you had a death threat from an angry listener or something?'

'Just listen to the start of the show, Andrew,' said Roman mysteriously, 'and all will be revealed.'

66

Roman settled himself behind his studio console, arranged the papers he needed—log, live copy, weather forecast, newspaper clippings—around him, and thought through what he would say on air.

As the nine o'clock news ended and his theme music started, Roman pressed the intercom button to the news booth and said to the newsreader, 'Gillian, listen to the opening of my show—I've got a story for you.'

She acknowledged the message by clicking the intercom button several times.

Then Roman faded down the theme music and began.

In somewhat purple prose he described his adventure of the evening: finding the body and calling the police. He omitted only four things: the reason for his appointment with the murdered businessman, the identity and nationality of the victim, and exactly where the murder had taken place.

Predictably, the first call he took on the talk-back was from a death-penalty nutter who was almost chortling over Roman's experience.

'Now you've seen a corpse with a knife in its back you've got to agree that locking up is too good for the animal that did the deed!'

'No,' said Roman, 'I don't. Because I don't believe that public policy should be based on emotion. Especially not on the emotions I obviously felt when confronted with a grim and frightening experience. Despite the shock to my nerves, my head still knows that, of all convicted criminals, murderers are the least likely to be repeat offenders.'

'You'll never learn, will you Roman?' growled the caller. 'You're a hopeless case!'

And with a loud clunk the phone was slammed down.

The next two callers were old ladies who wanted to sympathise with Roman over the shock he had been through and to pass on their recipes for homemade nerve soothing tonics.

During the commercial break that followed Andrew buzzed Roman to say, 'I've just had a call from the news editor at the *Telegraph-Mirror*. He heard the opening and he'd like to interview you about finding the corpse. He said he can do it over the telephone during the ten o'clock news.'

'I've got a better idea,' said Roman. 'Suggest that he talk to me on air. He can interview me on my own show. That will give him what he wants, and it should make an interesting bit of radio.'

Roman's producer conveyed this to the newspaper journalist who took nearly five mintues to agree to this unusual proposal.

The result was that immediately after the nine thirty news headlines Roman introduced his next talk-back caller as Carl Phillips from the *Tele-Mirror* and explained what was about to happen to the listeners. Then he handed it over to Phillips to ask the questions.

During the ten o'clock news both Andrew and Peter came into the studio asking for, as they put it, more of the 'gory details'.

Towards the end of the ten o'clock bulletin, Detective Fitzpatrick, who had been sitting in the lobby, tentatively poked his head around the studio door and asked if he might watch Roman at work.

'Sure,' said Roman. 'Come in and take a seat on the other side of the desk. But you'll find it pretty boring I'm afraid. You'll need to slip those headphones on so that you can hear the talk-back callers' side of the conversation as well as mine.'

The tone having been set by Roman's opening

remarks the talk-back callers wanted to discuss murder and violence. Before long the calls were focusing on violence in popular entertainment, and the effect of movies and videos in producing a more violent society.

During the eleven o'clock news a reporter from the *Sydney Morning Herald* rang and did a quick off-air interview with Roman, and Andrew came into the studio with the news that a woman named Liz had been frantically calling Roman for the past hour.

'Did she say what she wanted?' asked Roman.

'No. She just said it was personal and urgent. She's been practically pleading for you to call her back after you get off the air.'

'If she calls again, tell her I'll ring her just after midnight.'

Andrew left the room and Roman turned to the detective who was still in the guest chair in the studio.

'That's interesting, isn't it?' said Roman.

'I take it that's the woman who first got you involved in this business?' asked Fitzpatrick.

'That's her. If she's as upset as all that, she must have some news about Simon. Or perhaps she's spoken to Simon and what he's told her has distressed her? Anyway, we'll know the answer in just over an hour.'

As the evening wore on, the subjects raised by the talk-back callers became more varied. A woman rang to complain about her children being bullied at school and asked for advice on how they should handle it. Immediately the board lit up with callers keen to give her some. A woman rang to complain about the bullying of animals. She had been upset that afternoon to see a boy savagely beating a dog. In response another caller said some dogs deserved to be beaten, and went into a long story about her pekinese being attacked by a bull terrier.

Finally midnight came, Roman signed off the show, pushed his chair back from the desk and let out a long, audible sigh.

'A long day?' asked Fitzpatrick.

'You could say that,' replied Roman.

The studio door swung open and Andrew Gardner burst into the room with his usual excess of energy.

'You'd better ring up that woman, Mark,' he said. 'I'll pack up this mess.'

Roman looked around. Somehow he had managed to make the studio much messier than usual. Scraps of paper, old newspapers and discarded audio cartridges were scattered on every available surface.

'Thanks,' he muttered, and waved his hand around the mess saying, 'Sorry about all this.'

He walked down the corridor to his pokey little office with Fitzpatrick close behind him. Flinging his tall, solid frame into the one comfortable chair in the office he dialled Liz's number. It was answered almost immediately.

'It's Mark Roman here, Liz.'

'Oh, I'm so glad you rang! Bertram and I are so worried!'

'Tell me what's happened.'

'The police have taken Simon away,' she sobbed.

'What? Arrested him?' asked Roman looking up at the detective lounging in his office doorway and raising a querying eyebrow as he spoke. In response, Fitzpatrick shrugged non-committally.

'No. . .no. . .not arrested. . .I don't think so. They just wanted to ask him some questions. To help them with their inquiries they said. Oh, what does it mean, Mark?'

'Go back a bit, Liz. I rang for Simon just after seven and he wasn't there. When did he finally get home?'

'Nearly nine o'clock. And he was in a very strange mood. Very silent. He wouldn't answer our questions.'

'Did he tell you what happened at his office today?'

'No, what did happen?'

'Did he talk about a meeting he had?'

'He didn't mention any meeting. Mark, what's been happening?'

'When did the police come?' asked Roman, dodging her question.

'About ten o'clock.'

'And what did they say?'

'Nothing to us. They talked to Mark on the porch for a while, then he came inside and said he was going with them and would be back later. Mark, you know more about this than we do, don't you? I heard you talking about finding a dead body—is that what this is all about?'

'It might be. I didn't mention it on air, but the place where I found the corpse was in the office of Network Systems.'

As he spoke Roman looked up at the detective who stared back unblinkingly, as expressionless as a side of beef. But his presence intimidated Roman.

'Oh, Mark, I'm so worried—' began Liz, and then she stopped suddenly, 'Just a moment. . . I can hear the front door opening. . . let me go and see who it is. . .'

The phone clunked in Roman's ear as Liz's handpiece was dropped loudly. Then distant voices echoed from a corridor. One of them he was sure was Simon's, but he could only make out about one word in seven.

Eventually Liz returned to the phone. 'It's Simon,'

she said breathlessly. 'But he still wouldn't talk to me.'

'Tell him I'd like to have a word with him,' said Roman.

Again that loud clunk, and then the sound of Liz calling shrilly, 'Simon! Simon! Mark Roman would like to speak to you.'

There was a pause, a distant muffled reply, and then Liz was back. 'He's already on his way to his room. He says he's too tired to talk to anyone tonight, and he'll talk to us all in the morning.'

'Okay, I'll have a chat to him then.'

'Mark, do you know what this is all about?'

Roman glanced at Detective Fitzpatrick and replied, 'No, there's nothing I can tell you.'

'It's just that Simon has been through so much,' said Liz with a steady throb in her voice. 'He suffered a great deal of trauma as a child, you know.'

'I can imagine.'

'And that trauma could surface at any time. Anything could set it off. He could have a nervous breakdown you know.'

'Oh, I doubt that. Surely he's too young, too fit.'

'He could, Mark, he could. Think what he's been through: his mother murdered, his father a murderer, transplanted from one country to another at a young and sensitive age, then his father trying to manipulate him under his wing, and now the police are asking him questions about this dead body. What will happen next? Will his brother be murdered? Or me? Or his Uncle Bertram? Or Simon himself? Oh, Mark! Could Simon's life be at risk?'

'I don't know, Liz, but I seriously doubt it. You musn't allow yourself to become too worked up. Try to get a good night's rest. If you like I'll come around and see you in the morning.'

It took a good deal more talking on Roman's part to get Liz calmed down and off the phone, but eventually he succeeded.

A few minutes later Roman was behind the wheel of the Volvo, with Fitzpatrick beside him, pulling out of the radio station's basement car park.

As the roller door swung up, and Roman accelerated up the steep driveway, he was surprised to find that it was raining again. The hot, summer electrical storms had returned, and with them had come the rain. It was teeming down in steady, drenching sheets as Roman turned the car northwards again.

Conscious of the policeman beside him Roman drove slowly and cautiously through the heavy downpour. The constant drumming of the deluge drowned out all attempts at conversation.

Like all summer storms, it eased off as quickly as it began and, by the time they had reached the offices of Network Systems, there was little more than a misty drizzle. At half past twelve in the morning Roman was able to park in front of the main doors to the office block, so he left his umbrella in the car and he and Fitzpatrick sprinted through the sprinkling rain to the shelter of the lobby.

On the third floor all the lights were turned on and policemen were standing around talking in small groups.

'Ah, welcome back, Mr Roman,' said Kline when he saw him. 'How did the show go?'

'Fine, thanks. Can we get this over and done with? I'm starting to feel pretty tired.'

'Of course you are. This won't take long, just follow me.'

Kline led the way into the executive offices. Roman glanced at the desk at the end of the large room, but the body had been removed. For some reason the absence of the corpse was a relief, and he realised how tense he had been all evening.

'Now, Mr Roman,' said Kline—in a voice that implied 'I'm-being-patient-with-the-dummies'—'I'd like you to walk through your movements in this room when you came in and discovered the body.'

'Well. . . I came in through this far door here,' said Roman.

'Was it locked?'

'No. In fact, it might even have been slightly ajar I think. I'm not certain.'

'But it definitely wasn't locked?'

'No.'

'Okay, so you came in through the door. Why this office? How did you know to look here?'

'The other door was locked and the rest is all open plan. I could see it was deserted. This was the only place I hadn't looked.'

'Okay. Did you spot the body at once?'

'Almost at once. I came in calling out. . .'

'Calling out what?'

' "Hello, is anyone there?" Something like that.'

'And there was no reply, of course.'

'No reply.'

'Did you hear any sounds at all when you were walking through that empty office? Or when you came in here?'

'No. . . I don't think so. Why? Do you think the murderer might have still been there?'

Kline paused, as if wondering whether or not to tell him, and then said, 'The preliminary guess from the medical officer is that the man may have died—I stress *may*—just minutes before you found him.'

Roman felt his back muscles tense up again. Could

the murderer still have been on the third floor when he arrived? Had he come close to being murdered himself?

'Relax, Mr Roman,' said Kline, reading his thoughts. 'I doubt that you were ever at any risk. So, we have established that you heard nothing. When you saw the body on the desk—did you walk straight up to it?'

'Yes. I reached out and lifted one arm—which just flopped back. So then I walked around the desk and felt for a pulse in the wrist.'

'Was the hand still warm?'

'It's hard to say exactly. It certainly did not feel cold and clammy. I have never actually touched a dead body, at least not before tonight, so I have nothing to compare it with.'

'Just show me beside the desk exactly where you stood.'

The next fifteen minutes were occupied with Roman standing first here and then there, then showing how he had walked across to the coat rack. Had he touched anything else in the room? No, Roman was sure that he hadn't. The questions went over the same ground several times.

Finally Kline announced 'That's all, Mr Roman. You're free to go. If any other questions occur to us we'll be in touch.'

Roman escaped gratefully from the scene of the crime and more than that, from the hardened shell of non-reaction that Kline and Fitzpatrick displayed in the face of violent death. A protective shell, Roman assumed, that they had built up over many years.

Out on the street the rain had stopped again. The warm air was now completely still. It was a heavy damp stillness as though the world had stopped breathing.

Roman drove home to Kirribilli, tyres splashing through the slick of rainwater that covered the roads, parked his car at the kerb opposite his apartment, and, a moment later, shut his front door behind him with a sense of shutting out a world of worry.

After showering he prowled around the kitchenette for a while, but found the prospect of eating repulsive. Under the shower he had imagined that he would find it hard to sleep, but within ten minutes a great heaviness, an aching tiredness, came upon him. He lay on the bed and fell quickly and deeply asleep.

Roman's built-in body clock woke him at his usual hour of nine am. He drew back the bedroom curtains to find the clouds gone and a clear and blazing blue sky. The street surface was dry again, except for a few patches of heavy shadow where there were still a few puddles of unevaporated rainwater.

The warm, sticky humidity was as dense as an invasion of ectoplasm. Roman was gleaming with sweat, as if he had been digging ditches in his sleep. He had another quick cold shower before dressing, shaving and setting the coffee percolator into action.

As he took his regular morning walk up to the Kirribilli shops, he found himself trying to block out thoughts of the previous night. But there were some questions that insisted on invading his mind. Had Simon murdered his brother? If so, what possible motive could there be? And if not, who had arrived between Simon's departure and Roman's arrival to murder Salvador Escobar? And why?

The newsagent greeted him with a broad grin. 'You've made it onto the front page this morning, Mr Roman.'

Roman picked up a *Tele-Mirror* and read the lead headline: RADIO STAR FINDS BODY.

'Must have been quite a shock, Mr Roman,' continued the newsagent.

'Yes. . .yes it was,' muttered Roman as he hurriedly paid his sixty cents and escaped.

At the baker's he ordered his usual hot bread rolls, and was aware of stares from the other customers as he was being served. They too had read the headlines.

Back in the apartment he spread out the paper and quickly scanned it while breakfasting.

Under the big RADIO STAR headline were several paragraphs that reported his finding of the corpse and calling the police and then a slug that said 'continued on page 2'.

The second front page headline read: SYDNEY SWELTERS — HOTTEST DECEMBER IN TEN YEARS. Underneath was a photograph of two very small, and very cute, children paddling at Manly beach.

Roman turned to page two. There was a photograph of himself beside the continuation of the story. He groaned out loud—it was the same old publicity shot they insisted on using. It was so old that his thick hair was black instead of grey. The radio station had sent them more recent photos but for some reason this was the one that always came out of the file.

He read the half a dozen paragraphs of text beside his photograph. The police had still not released the name of the victim ('not until relatives have been notified') and there was nothing there that Roman did not already know.

He stacked the breakfast dishes in the sink, slipped on his sunglasses, picked up the keys, and walked down to his car.

As he drove towards Wollstonecraft he noticed that

the traffic was slower than usual, as if sapped of energy by the burning, furnace-like sun.

He decided not to park the car in the unshaded driveway of the Miller house, and, instead, propped it in the street in a large pool of shade under an old peppercorn tree.

He had to stand on the Miller doorstep for several minutes, and ring the bell twice, before the door swung slowly open.

'Good morning, Mr Roman, won't you come in?' said Bertram, standing back and opening the door wide.

Roman stepped thankfully into the cool, dim interior of the old house. 'How is Liz this morning?' he asked.

'She's had very little sleep, I'm afraid,' said Bertram, leading the way not to the little sitting room where Roman had been the day before, but further down the corridor towards the back of the house.

'Come into the breakfast room, Mr Roman,' said Bertram opening a door and standing back. 'We call it the breakfast room but nowadays we eat all our meals in here.'

It was a long, narrow room. At one end was a small, round dining table with a set of four dining chairs. Further along was a sideboard, a sofa, and two armchairs. On the sideboard was a silver coffee pot, a silver milk jug and a sugar caddy.

'The coffee is still fresh,' said Bertram from behind Roman's back, 'Would you like a cup?'

'That would be nice, yes please.'

'If you'll wait a moment I'll fetch a cup from the kitchen.'

As Bertram departed Roman looked slowly around the room. It was as cluttered with bric-a-brac as the small sitting room had been. On the sideboard, beside the coffee pot, was a framed wedding photograph of Liz and Bertram, a commemorative plate on a stand, an old radio-cassette player (possibly the radio they listen to my show on, thought Roman), a telephone, and a china figurine of a shepherdess.

Bertram returned with a large cup and saucer in a faded willow pattern design. Roman helped himself to coffee, milk and sugar.

He was sipping the coffee when Liz spoke from the doorway behind him.

'Thank you for coming, Mark,' she said, in a faint, trembling voice.

Roman turned around and was shocked by the change he saw. Liz's eyes were red from weeping, her hair had not been brushed, and her skin, devoid this morning of any make-up looked almost grey it was so pale.

'You don't look at all well, Liz,' said Roman.

'Oh, don't worry about me,' she said, waving away his concern. 'It's Simon we need to worry about.'

'What has he told you this morning?' asked Roman, and then, much to his embarrassment, she began to cry.

'Nothing,' she wept. 'He still refuses to tell me anything, or explain anything.'

She pulled out a sodden handkerchief, blew her nose, sniffled several times, and then said, 'I'm sorry about carrying on like this, Mark.'

'It's all right,' said Roman. 'I can understand that you must be very worried.'

'What can you tell me about what has happened, Mark? Why did those policemen want to talk to Simon? It's to do with that dead body you found, isn't it?'

'Yes. Have the police told you the identity of the murdered man yet?'

'No, no they haven't.'

'Has Simon?'

'No, he hasn't either,' said Liz sullenly. 'Doesn't he realise what he's putting me through?'

'Probably not,' said Roman. 'He has a lot on his mind at the moment.'

'Do *you* know, Mark? Can you tell me?'

'I think I had better. The police might not like it, but it seems cruel to leave you wondering like this. You know that an official from the headquarters of Earthfast in Ecuador is visiting the Sydney office at the moment?'

'Yes,' sniffled Liz into her damp handkerchief. 'Simon told me that the night before last.'

'Well, that's the man who was killed, the man whose body I found in the office last night.'

'But . . . but, there's more to it than that, isn't there?'

'Yes, there is. This man from Ecuador, the man from head office who was murdered last night, was Simon's brother, Salvador Escobar.'

Liz's response was a sharp intake of breath. 'Are you sure?' she asked, her eyes wide with astonishment. 'Are you quite certain?'

'I saw his passport photo. It's him all right.'

'I see.'

There was a long silence. Liz stared blindly into the distance. Her face was blotchy now, looking as though she had been hit, and she looked ten years older than when Roman had first seen her, only the day before.

'I see,' she said again, 'but I don't really understand.'

'Neither do I,' said Roman in his quietest, most sympathetic voice. He knew that in difficult and emotional situations he sometimes started using microphone tricks—dropping his voice half an octave and making it husky. It was an artificiality he disliked in himself, but it was a habit he found hard to break.

'How did Salvador die?' asked Liz quietly.

Roman was surprised for a moment to hear her refer to the dead man by his first name. But of course, Roman reminded himself, Salvador Escobar was Liz and Bertram's nephew, and they had known him as a child.

'How did he die?' she asked. 'You keep saying murder, but is there any possibility that it was an accident?'

'No chance at all. He was stabbed in the back.'

'Oh. I see.'

There was another long silence. Roman waited patiently for Liz to speak.

'But why is Simon involved?' she asked at length, 'Why are the police talking to him?'

'Well, it looks as though he may have been the last person to see Salvador Escobar alive. Apart from the murderer that is. I happen to know that Simon and Salvador had an appointment last night at half past five. How long that meeting went on I don't know. If Salvador was pleading a case on behalf of his father it may have lasted some considerable time—perhaps an hour or more. I arrived at a few minutes past seven, and it appears that Escobar was murdered just before I got there.'

'Do you think the police suspect Simon of the murder?'

'Surely not,' said Roman. 'What motive could there possibly be?'

'Yes. Exactly. Simon is safe, he must be safe. The police could never arrest him without a motive, and there is no motive.'

'Has Simon said anything? Anything at all?'

'No.'

'So you have no idea what happened at that meeting between Simon and his long lost brother?'

'I wish I did, I just wish I did,' said Liz fervently.

'Whatever it was, it must have upset Simon a lot, musn't it?'

'It would have been a pack of lies,' snapped Liz with a sudden flash of fire. 'He must have been peddling the same old lies that his father always tells.'

'Whatever it was, it was enough to. . .to what? Well, to stun Simon into silence, I suppose. And then before he could recover and talk to you about it, the police came. The news of Salvador's death was the second shock. And if he got the impression that the police suspected him of the murder that would have been yet another shock. Perhaps his reluctance to talk about it just yet is understandable.'

'But he has always talked to us, to Bertram and me. He's never kept anything from us.'

'Still, a series of shocks in a row like that. I know there are times,' said Roman, 'when I just want to withdraw from people for a while and be by myself.'

'But not Simon,' insisted Liz. 'He's not like that.'

The unfinished coffee in Simon's cup had gone cold, and he put it down on the sideboard, next to the telephone.

'Perhaps,' suggested Liz, 'perhaps he would talk to you?'

'I doubt it,' said Roman, 'I doubt it very much. If he won't talk to his own family he certainly won't talk to me.'

'But perhaps we are too close to him, Bertram and me, and perhaps he would find it easier to talk to someone he doesn't actually live with. Try for me Mark, please? I'm going to keep on worrying until I know what the police said to him last night. It's sheer torment not knowing what they said and whether they suspect him or not. Try and talk to him for me, please?'

Roman thought for a moment, and then, more because of his need to understand the situation than because of Liz's plea he said, 'All right. I'll try. Where will I find him? I suppose he'll be in his office by now?'

'Oh no. He didn't go to work today. He's still upstairs in his room. You can see him right now. Bertram will show you the way.'

Chapter 5

Roman found Bertram in the corridor, just outside the breakfast room door. Almost as though he was waiting to be summoned by Liz.

Bertram led the way up to a flight of stairs and directed Roman to a bedroom on the right. The stairs were covered in a worn red carpet, and had finely turned handrails in a dark, polished timber.

Roman rapped sharply on the door. 'Simon, it's Mark. May I have a word?'

For a minute or so he suspected that he was going to be ignored. Then he heard a shuffle inside the room, the lock clicked, and the door swung open.

Simon was dressed in T-shirt and jeans, his hair was uncombed and he needed a shave.

'Can I come in?'

'We can talk here,' said Simon curtly.

'You know that I discovered the body last night?'

'Yes. The police told me.'

'And in the process I discovered his identity. He was—'

'My long lost brother! Yes, so I learned yesterday.'

'You didn't know that earlier in the day, when we were talking in the coffee lounge?'

'No. If I had I would have told you,' snapped Simon.

'Was it a shock?'

'What? Meeting my brother?'

'Yes.'

'Not much of a shock. Not really. I had always known he was there in Ecuador. And I knew he worked for my father—our father, I should say. I suppose I had assumed that there was a chance that I would meet him someday.'

'Why did the police want to interview you last night?'

'Because they think I was the last person to see him, Salvador, alive. But you know that—you told them.'

'Are you suggesting that I shouldn't have?' asked Roman defensively.

'Of course not,' replied Simon with a shrug of his shoulders.

'Do the police suspect you of the murder?'

A cloud came over Simon's face as though this was a possibility that had not occurred to him before.

'Suspect me? I don't think so. Why should they?'

'What did they want to know?'

'When my meeting with Salvador began, when it ended, what we talked about, what sort of mood he was in. The sort of questions I imagine they always ask in a murder case.'

'When did the meeting end? How long were you with your brother?'

'It lasted about an hour. Maybe a little more. I think it was just after half past six when I left him.'

'And yet you didn't get home until after nine o'clock

last night: what were you doing between six thirty and nine?'

Simon turned away from Roman and looked back into his room for a while before answering. 'Just thinking. I went for a drive. I wanted to be by myself to sort things out in my head.'

'Where did you drive to?'

'Down to Balls Head Reserve. I parked the car and sat on a bench looking at the harbour. I stayed there until it was completely dark.'

'What were you thinking about?'

'No offence, Mr Roman, but that's really none of your business.'

'I'm sorry, I don't mean to intrude. But I found the body and, like it or not, I'm involved.'

'Maybe so. But there are still some things that I'm not interested in talking about.'

'Is that why you're not talking to Liz and Bertram? Can't you discuss this with your own aunt and uncle?'

'It's been a shock, Mr Roman,' said Simon, 'Haven't you ever wanted to be alone when you've had a shock? I will talk to Aunt Liz and Uncle Bertram, but not now. Later.'

'Have you any idea who might have wanted to kill your brother?'

'None at all.'

'When you were with him, was he apprehensive, did you get the impression that he was aware of being in danger?'

'No, not in the least.'

'Did he mention another appointment after yours? Someone else he was going to see?'

'He didn't mention anything of the sort. In our conversation we were very focused on what we had to talk about.'

'And what did you talk about?'

'Family matters. Is that everything you wanted to ask?' Simon started to close his door.

'There is just one other question. But I am reluctant to ask it; I don't want to give offence.'

'Ask anything you want, Mr Roman.'

'Did you murder your brother?'

'No, Mr Roman, I did not.' With that Simon's door closed firmly in Roman's face and the lock clicked.

Roman walked back downstairs slowly, lost in thought.

Liz was waiting for him at the foot of the stairs.

'Well?' she asked, 'What did you find out?'

'Very little, I'm afraid. Nothing significant.'

Liz put her sodden handkerchief up to her mouth, sobbed once, and then wiped her nose.

'In fact, the situation is just as I guessed it might be,' said Roman. 'He's upset and he wants some time alone to sort himself out. He'll talk to you—just give him time.'

Liz thanked Roman for his help, and Bertram showed him to the front door.

As he stepped out of the porch and onto the gravel driveway the air sizzled and the glare made Roman squint and feel for his sunglasses.

He walked back to his car, still absorbed in his thoughts. How much of Simon's story should he believe? The young man had two-and-a-half hours of time unaccounted for, except to say that he was 'thinking'.

Had Simon's meeting with his brother become so distressing that it had ended in murder? Had, for instance, the issue of their mother's murder come up? Had Salvador said something that Simon found unforgivable, and had an argument ended in violence?

If Simon was guilty of the murder that would certainly account for his strange behaviour.

While Roman had been inside the house the sun had shifted and the shadow of the peppercorn tree was no longer sheltering the Volvo. When Roman unlocked the driver's door he was hit once again with a gust of hot air.

With the air-conditioning on high, he started driving home, but after several blocks had another idea. When he hit the Pacific Highway he turned left and headed north.

Simon, he remembered, had yesterday described his meeting with Salvador Escobar as a meeting for coffee. What if they didn't meet in the office, but went to a coffee lounge instead? In that case, the most likely place was the coffee lounge where Roman had met Simon yesterday.

At the Crows Nest business centre Roman parked in a side street and walked one block up the highway towards the Network Systems building. As he walked, bright splashes of sunlight bounced off car windscreens and glass-fronted buildings and into his eyes like camera flashes.

He stepped into the coffee lounge's air-conditioning with relief and was pleased to see that the same pale waitress was on duty.

Turning his back on the street glare he walked to the rear of the coffee lounge and took a seat. The waitress ambled slowly across, her eyes as glazed as a flathead in a fishshop window.

'Can I take your order sir?'

'A Vienna coffee please.'

'Anything to eat with that, sir?' (All of these waitresses, thought Roman, have been programmed by the same American computer.)

'Just the coffee, thanks.'

Several minutes later she returned with the foaming, creamy cup of coffee. 'Will that be all, sir?'

'Just a question or two, if I may?' said Roman in his warmest, commercial-reading voice, flashing a smile as he spoke.

The waitress raised an eyebrow, said nothing, and waited.

'What time do you finish here in the evenings?'

This time the expression on her face registered an encyclopedic range of astonishment and Roman realised that he had been misunderstood. 'Hang on, I expressed that badly. What I mean is, some friends of mine were due to meet here at half past five yesterday, would you still have been on duty then?'

'Oh. Well, yes. I work till seven.'

'Do you remember me coming here in the middle of the afternoon with a young man?'

'Sure. I recognised you, Mr Roman.'

'Good. The young man I was with, did he come back with another man at half past five?'

'Yeah...yeah...he did. I remember.'

'What did the other man look like?'

'Dark. Sort of Italian. Or Lebanese.'

'You didn't happen to hear any of their conversation did you?'

'I don't listen to customers' conversations!'

'No, of course not. But this happens to be very important. I'm trying to help a friend who could be in serious trouble,' said Roman, turning on every ounce of charm he could muster, 'and I would be very appreciative if you could recall anything, anything at all.'

'Well, I couldn't really hear what they were saying, but I did notice that they got a bit worked up.'

'Tell me about it.'

'At first the other man, not your friend—the dark man—just talked and talked and talked and your friend listened. And then they argued.'

'Argued? Are you sure?'

'Sure I'm sure.'

'What did they argue about?'

'I don't know, they argued in whispers. But they were sure worked up about it.'

'I see. And did you happen to notice what time either of them left?'

'They left together, Mr Roman, at about half past six I think.'

'Thank you very much, you've been very helpful.'

The waitress had emerged sufficiently from her stupor to smile prettily in response to Roman's thanks, then she ambled her slow way back to the cappuccino bar near the door.

Roman drank his coffee in a thoughtful silence. So far he had been trying to absorb the situation, the people and their relationships, like a sponge, now he had to start thinking about what he had absorbed.

Simon Miller and Salvador Escobar had argued yesterday, and then they had left the coffee lounge together. What had they argued about? Were they still arguing when they left, or had they resolved their differences by then? And how long did they stay together after they left the coffee lounge? According to Simon's account they split up almost at once, but was he telling the truth?

Roman's mind was still buzzing with questions as he drove back down the highway, turned left at Falcon Street, left again at Alexander Street and propped the car in the council car park. Then he walked back to Falcon Street and entered the pleasant shadowed interior of the Bravo Italian restaurant, coffee bar, and gelato bar.

Roman did not feel like a heavy lunch, so instead of going upstairs to the restaurant he sat downstairs in the coffee bar and ordered a small pasta dish— tortellini with mushroom and cream sauce—and followed that with a helping of the Bravo's legendary gelato.

After lunch he returned through the sauna that was Sydney in this unseasonable December to his apartment at Kirribilli.

Stripped to his underwear, and with the ceiling fan slowly revolving overhead, Roman paced backwards and forwards in the small space his living room allowed trying to decide what to do next.

He felt like someone in a large, dark room with a small flashlight. Whatever happened to fall within its small circle of light he could see and understand, but he could get no idea of the shape of the whole room.

He decided to let his subconscious wrestle with the problem of the murder of Salvador Escobar for a while, and turned to the daily routine of preparing his evening talk-back show. The next hour was occupied by careful scrutiny of the newspaper, clipping selected items and scribbling down notes about them.

At the end of the hour he fixed himself a cold drink (half orange juice and half Perrier), and sat back in an armchair. As he sipped his drink and fanned himself with the tattered remnants of the newspaper he discovered that, while his conscious mind had been preoccupied, his subconscious had indeed made some progress.

As a result, he could now see that he had been looking at only part of the equation. While he had come to some sort of understanding of the Miller family he knew almost nothing about the Escobars. What's more he really wanted to get some idea of how the police were looking at the case, and what they had found out.

Roman grabbed his telephone to see what he could discover with a few phone calls.

He dialled the number of his own radio station, asked to be put through to the newsroom, and then asked for Brian Farrell, the station's police roundsman.

'Brian? It's Mark Roman here.'

'G'day, Mark. What can I do for you, old son?'

'You know about the body I found last night?'

'I sure do. I went through the tape of your opening remarks from last night's show to find a bit of eyewitness account to put in the breakfast news.'

'Sorry, Brian, I should have thought to leave you a voicer on tape.'

'It was no trouble, mate, I found a nice bit easily enough and I did my own wrap-around from what police PR told me.'

'Good. Look, I'm ringing to ask a favour.'

'I guessed as much, fire away.'

'I'd like to find out more about this murder, since I am personally involved as it were.'

'As the corpse-finder you mean?'

'Precisely. Could you use your contacts to put me in touch with a policeman who could tell me—off the record of course—what their scientific people found at the scene and where the investigation is up to, and that sort of thing?'

'Tricky. I know one or two people who'd tell *me*, but it takes a while to build up a level of trust. Still, they will have heard you on the air, and they will know from your editorials that you are pro-police not anti-police, and if I vouch for you, we might be able to manage something. Who is in charge, do you know?'

'A couple of detectives named Kline and Fitzpatrick—Jim Kline and Ian Fitzpatrick.'

'Don't know them. It was at Crows Nest where you found the body wasn't it?'

'That's right.'

'They'll be from North Sydney police station then, my contacts there are not very good.'

'Well, it was worth a try anyway.'

'Hang on. Don't give up just yet, mate. My best contact in the force is Bob Lineham—he's a DS in Serious Crime.'

'Translate that last bit for me, Brian.'

'Lineham is a Detective Sergeant in the Serious Crime Squad. I'm on my way back to Police Head-quarters now for the afternoon briefing, and I'll pop in and have a word with Bob. If he knows anything, or can find out anything, I think he might be willing to have a chat to you.'

'Thanks for that, Brian. I'll hear from you then, will I?'

'I'll call, where will you be?'

Roman gave Brian Farrell his home number and rang off.

He immediately dialled the same number again, asked to be put through to the newsroom, and this time asked for Robyn Hardy, the station's business and finance reporter.

'Robyn? It's Mark Roman, how are you? Listen, have you got a few minutes to spare?'

'Sure. What's the problem?'

'I want a bit of background information on a topic that falls onto your patch.'

'Happy to help. What do you want to know?'

'About a company called Earthfast—have you heard of them?'

'Sure. I did a major piece on them when they started setting up their Australian retail chain around three years ago. And I do pieces on them from time to time in my international finance report.'

'Do you know much about the man who set up the company?'

'Raffael Escobar? I know what's generally known, that's all. He's an interesting man.'

'Give me a run down.'

'Well, where do I begin? Hang on, let me go to my files, I've got a profile piece on him somewhere that I clipped out of the *Financial Review* last year.'

Robyn put the phone down on the desk and for several minutes all Roman could hear coming down the line was the general buzz of the newsroom.

'Are you still there, Mark?' asked Robyn picking up the phone.

'I'm still here.'

'Sorry about the delay, my filing cabinet's a bit of a mess. Anyway I found the clipping, do you want me to run through the highlights?'

'Yes please.'

'Well, let me see. Raffael Escobar was born in Ecuador as the heir of one of the great aristocratic families of that country. Apparently he is descended from Spanish nobility and can trace his family back more generations than you've had hot dinners.'

'I presume that means he was born rich.'

'You presume right. And not just rich, very rich. Just a sec while I run my eye down this a bit further. It appears he was not only rich but smart with it— he has degrees from universities in Quito, Madrid and Paris.'

'What did he study?'

'Let's see. It says here engineering, architecture and design.'

'Okay, what else?'

'When he finished his studies, instead of taking over the management of the family's plantations and other investments, he became an artist.'

'An artist?'

'That's right. A sculptor to be precise. After several exhibitions in the United States, with considerable success, he turned his talents to creating employment and export income for Ecuador.'

'This is the furniture thing?'

'Yes. The company was originally called Escobar Designer Furniture and it was a great success almost from the beginning. Raffael Escobar drew all the designs himself using the timbers and native products of Ecuador. He designed the buildings that house his factory, he managed the company, he did everything.'

'What sort of furniture is it?'

'Very classy, and it found a special niche at the top of the market in Europe and America and later here. A few years after he founded the company he changed the name to Earthfast to emphasise the environmentally friendly nature of the product—plantation grown timber, all natural fabrics, that sort of thing.'

'How long has he operated in Australia?'

'Well the furniture has been sold here for over twenty years, but a few years ago he did what he has done in other countries and set up a chain of specialist stores to sell his furniture. They are not big stores, and they are only in the major cities, but they give him what we financial reporters call vertical integration.'

'I'm sure you could explain that if I asked you to, Robyn.'

'What it means is—'

'No, don't bother! It's not the financial side I'm interested in.'

'That's the big picture anyway. I don't think there's much more I can tell you.'

'Is there anything there about his personal life?'

'Not much. Just a sec. Ah, yes, here we are. He was married, to an Australian girl as it happens, but she died some seventeen years ago and he has never re-married. That's about all the personal information there is. Does that help?'

'Not enough actually. You see, it's not so much his private life that I want to know about as him as a person. What is his personality? What is he like?'

'That I can't help you with. You need a report from a psychologist not a business journalist.'

'But in the absence of that psychological profile, does that clipping in front of you say anything about what type of man he is? What is his reputation like?'

'Well. . . let's see. . . it does say something about his reputation as an employer.'

'What exactly?'

'Apparently he has an absolutely top reputation as an employer—better even than the Japanese or Swedish companies. Down near the end of this piece here it says that he provides health care and education for his factory workers and their families. And accommodation too in a housing development he has built near his factory in Guayaquil, which is a model of its kind. He even has what is described as 'the most generous retirement plan in the world' for the older workers. Does any of that information help?'

'It just might, Robyn. Thanks for that.'

'If you like I can photocopy this whole report and leave it in your pigeon-hole.'

'Yes, yes that's a good idea. That would be great if you'd do that.'

'No trouble. It will be waiting for you when you come in tonight.'

Roman thanked Robyn Hardy for all her help and hung up.

As he leaned back in his armchair and closed his eyes, trying to absorb all the information he had just heard, Roman realised that what he would like to see was a photograph of Raffael Escobar. He would like to see what sort of character was marked on the man's face and what message came from his eyes.

Roman tried to tease out what he had learned about this man, this father of both Simon—the suspect—and Salvador—the victim. Aristocratic, wealthy, highly educated, creative, inventive, a clever business man, a generous employer.

This was a side of Raffael Escobar that Roman had heard nothing of from Liz. How did those two sides fit together? And what was the son, Salvador Escobar, the murdered man, really like? Did he take after his father? And if so, in what ways?

Roman's whirling thoughts were interrupted by the ringing telephone. He grabbed it quickly, hoping it was Brian Farrell.

'Hello?'

'Mark? It's Hugh Marsden here.' Hugh was the minister of Roman's church, St Thomas' at North Sydney.

'Afternoon, Hugh. What can I do for you?'

'I'm sorry about the short notice, but Carols by Candlelight at North Sydney oval this Saturday night—can you do one of the Bible readings?'

'Sure, that's no problem.'

'I've been meaning to speak to you about it for a

couple of weeks but other things just crowded it out of my mind. Sorry about that . . . How are you coping with getting caught up in a murder case?'

'Fine. It's given me a bit of running around to do, that's all.'

'You're not getting stressed out?'

'No. Not yet anyway.'

'Why don't you come to lunch on Sunday, Jill and the kids would like that, and it's a while since you've had a meal with us.'

'I'd love to. What time?'

'One o'clock. How would that be?'

'Fine. I'll see you at one on Sunday. Now this Saturday night thing, when and where is that?'

'There's a stage that's being set up on the southern side of North Sydney oval, and the carol singing will start at seven thirty and be over by nine. Your Bible reading is almost in the middle of the program.'

'Okay. Now hang on while I grab a piece of paper, and you can give me the reading.' Roman found an old shopping list, turned it over to scribble on the back, and pulled out his pen. 'Okay. Fire away.'

'It's Luke chapter two,' said Hugh, 'verses one to twenty. You got that?'

'Got it. I'll see you on Saturday night then.'

'See you then.'

Roman was quite often asked to read the Bible, either in church or at special functions, because, as a radio man, he had the ability to read fluently and had a distinctively deep and mellow voice.

Roman walked over to the one small bookshelf in the room and there, at the end of a row of golf books, was his Good News Bible. While he was waiting for Brian Farrell to call back he might as well practise the reading. Roman was a great believer in rehearsing

carefully any Bible passage he had to read aloud.
He flipped open his Bible and read:

At that time the Emperor Augustus ordered a
census to be taken throughout the Roman Empire.
When this first census took place, Quirinius was
the governor of Syria. Everyone, then, went to
register himself, each to his own town.

Joseph went from the town of Nazareth in Galilee
to the town of Bethlehem in Judea, the birthplace
of King David. Joseph went there because he was
a descendant of David. He went to register with
Mary, who was promised in marriage to him. She
was pregnant, and while they were in Bethlehem,
the time came for her to have her baby. She gave
birth to her first son, wrapped him in strips of cloth
and laid him in a manger—there was no room for
them to stay at the inn.

There were some shepherds in that part of the
country who were spending the night in the fields,
taking care of their flocks. An angel of the Lord
appeared to them, and the glory of the Lord shone
over them. They were terribly afraid, but the angel
said to them, 'Don't be afraid! I am here with good
news for you, which will bring great joy to all the
people. This very day in David's town your Saviour
was born—Christ the Lord! And this is what will
prove it to you: you will find a baby wrapped in
strips of cloth and lying in a manger.'

Suddenly a great army of heaven's angels
appeared with the angel, singing praises to God:
'Glory to God in the highest heaven, and peace
on earth to those with whom he is pleased!'

When the angels went away from them back into
heaven, the shepherds said to one another, 'Let's

go into Bethlehem and see this thing that has happened, which the Lord has told us.'

So they hurried off and found Mary and Joseph and saw the baby lying in the manger. When the shepherds saw him, they told them what the angels had said about the child. All who heard it were amazed at what the shepherds said. Mary remembered all these things and thought deeply about them. The shepherds went back, singing praises to God for all they had heard and seen; it had been just as the angel had told them.

Roman put down the Bible and thought about the passage for a minute. He would have to think of some way to introduce this old story from a new angle, he realised. So, what could he say about it to modern, skeptical people who come out to Carols by Candlelight just as a family outing?

His thinking about that problem was interrupted by the telephone. It was Brian Farrell.

'There's a coffee shop in College Street, not far from police headquarters,' said Farrell. 'If you can be there in half an hour Bob Lineham and I can meet you there.'

Roman took down the directions, and headed for his car.

Chapter 6

Roman parked the Volvo at the War Memorial end of the Hyde Park side of College Street, locked the car, fed the meter, and looked around for the coffee shop where he was to meet Farrell. He found it almost opposite, just a few doors south of the police department's Avery Building.

Farrell was waiting at a back table, and stood up as Roman approached.

'G'day Mark. This is Bob Lineham—Bob, Mark Roman.'

Lineham was a broad-shouldered, solidly built man with a face that could have been carved out of ironbark. He was one of those men who go almost completely bald in their early thirties, and the only hair on his bullet-shaped head was a closely cropped fringe above his ears. After the formalities were over, and the coffee ordered, he spoke up.

'Jim Kline is an old mate of mine, so I've had a chat to him and I can tell you a bit. I've told him I'm meeting you and he knows what information I'll be passing on.'

The voice was quiet, with an odd sandpapery quality to it. 'We like to keep our friends in the media happy. Maybe someday you can do us a favour—'

'I'll owe you one,' said Roman.

'But you must understand,' continued the detective, 'that this is an off-the-record background briefing and is not to be quoted. Okay?'

'Understood.'

'All right. You ask the questions, some of which I'll be able to answer, and some of which I won't.'

'Okay,' said Roman. 'First, I guess, is the cause of death. Did he die from the obvious—from the stab wound, that is?'

'Yes. It went in through the back between the fourth and fifth ribs and into the heart.'

'Indicating anatomical knowledge?'

'Perhaps. Or, perhaps, indicating luck—or the sort of knowledge you can pick up in the average crime novel these days. The paperback shelf at your local newsagent contains all you need to know about murder.'

'And the time of death?'

'The autopsy confirmed the doctor's initial guess. Based on body temperature, and the degree of ingestion of coffee and buns that the deceased had consumed at around five-thirty, he must have died no more than ten minutes before you found him. Maximum.'

'Were there any other wounds on the body?'

Lineham's eyes opened fractionally beyond his usual slit-like glare.

'That's an intelligent question, Mr Roman,' he said.

'Are you allowed to answer it?'

'Certainly. There was a wound indicating a heavy blow to the back of the head.'

'Inflicted before or after death?'

'Shortly before.'

'So the murderer hit Salvador Escobar on the back of the head, and then stabbed him in the back?'

'Exactly.'

'Would the blow to the head have knocked him out?'

'It would almost certainly have rendered him unconscious.'

'Why? Why hit someone over the head, and *then* stab them in the back?'

'You draw your own conclusions, Mr Roman. I'll answer your questions, but I won't draw conclusions for you.'

'Perhaps the blow on the head was an attempt at murder, and the stab wound followed because the blow did not prove fatal?' suggested Roman.

'That's one possibility.'

'Or perhaps the preliminary blow on the head was to avoid a struggle?'

'That's another possibility.'

'Did they find the weapon he was hit with?'

'Indeed they did: it's a heavy glass paperweight.'

'No fingerprints?'

'Quite right—no fingerprints.'

'Was that paperweight something that was normally in the office? Or did the murderer bring it with him?'

'It had sat on that particular executive desk for over twelve months.'

'I see,' said Roman, rubbing his chin thoughtfully. 'And what about the knife? Has that been identified?'

'It has. Not a knife, but a letter-opener—with an unusual decorative handle.'

'Does that mean they know where the letter-opener came from?'

'Yes. It usually sat on the desk of Simon Miller.'

'Simon? Hmmm. I can see why he is being regarded as a suspect.'

'No one has said that he is a suspect at this stage, Mr Roman.'

'Well,' said Roman, looking sharply at Detective Lineham, 'let me ask you then: is he?'

'Pass. That's one of the questions I can't answer.'

'I see. But he was the last man to see the victim alive, and the murder weapon came from his desk. So it would be reasonable to include him on a list of suspects.'

Lineham paused before replying, 'It would be reasonable.'

'All you would need would be a motive?'

'We wouldn't proceed without a motive, that's true.'

'Tell me, in any murder inquiry—not just this case, but any case—how do you compile a list of suspects?'

'We look at family, at business associates, and social connections—pretty much in that order.'

'And that's what's happening in this case?'

'Procedures are being followed.'

'I'm not going to get much further asking you about suspects, am I?'

'No further at all, in fact,' agreed Lineham.

'Let's go back to this blow on the head then. Was it a high blow? I mean, was it struck from above?'

'It was.'

'That means the murderer was taller than Salvador Escobar?' said Roman (remembering that Simon was a tall young man).

'That's one possibility.'

'Only a possibility, you say? In that case. . .it is also a possibility. . .that the victim was seated and the murderer was standing behind him when he struck!'

'Well done, Mr Roman. That is certainly another possibility.'

'So was the murder unpremeditated? I mean, since both the paperweight and the letter-opener were weapons found on the spot, could the murder have been unplanned?'

'It could have been.'

'What other option is there?'

'There is the possibility that the murderer brought a weapon with him but decided to use the readily available weapons instead.'

'For what reason?'

'Weapons can be traced back to owners. Weapons picked up on the spot pose no such risk.'

'I see. And is that the way the investigative team is thinking at the moment?'

'I'm not telling you how anyone is thinking, Mr Roman,' said Lineham firmly. 'I'm just explaining some of the possibilities suggested by the facts.'

'Yes, yes, of course,' agreed Roman hastily.

At this point the detective started glancing at his wrist-watch, Roman got the message, and the meeting broke up shortly afterwards.

Back in his car, and heading down the Cahill Expressway, Roman flicked on the radio to hear that Sydney was heading for 'the hottest Christmas on record'. In response he turned the car air-conditioning up a notch higher.

The Volvo pulled out of the tight curves of the Cahill Expressway tunnel, and the Sydney Harbour Bridge loomed up ahead. Roman had been known to describe it on his program as 'the most beautiful steelwork on earth', and there was something about the bridge's combination of gracefully sweeping lines and massive riveted supports, that took Roman's breath away whenever he really looked at it.

The toot of a car horn from behind told Roman that he had slowed down to look, and he pushed his foot further down onto the accelerator.

As he travelled north Roman's mind returned to the Carols by Candlelight Bible reading. And he discovered that while he and Detective Lineham had been pre-occupied with violent death, his unconscious mind had solved the problem of how to introduce the reading.

With the words of the Bible passage rolling through his mind like a script through an auto-cue, he saw clearly that he should make just three quick comments to the crowd before he read that passage aloud.

The first was that the story was historical. The passage carefully anchors the events in history and geography with references to the Roman Emperor and the local Roman governor of the time and quite specific geographical information: this is *reporting* not *invention*.

The second was that the story was supernatural. Lots of people nowadays, Roman realised, feel uncomfortable with the notion of the supernatural. But this passage, with its angel messengers, brazenly advertises that God's intervention in human affairs is a spectacularly supernatural event.

And third, that the story was universal. The message of 'great joy to *all* the people' indicates that when God chooses to intervene in human affairs it is of massive, mind-blowing, cosmic significance.

Yes, thought Roman, that's what I'll say.

He turned off the expressway at Falcon Street. There was probably a later turn-off that was even closer to the Network Systems building, but he was uncertain which it was.

During his conversation with Detective Lineham a part of his mind, possibly his over-active unconscious, had decided that he needed to return to the Network Systems office—to absorb the atmosphere, to understand the people and their relationships.

From Falcon Street he drove up the Pacific Highway and parked in a side street at the St Leonard's end of Crows Nest.

The third floor receptionist was on the phone when he stepped out of the lift, and while he was waiting Roman managed to lean forward far enough to reach a sheet of Network Systems stationery. Underneath the letter-head were the words, 'General Manager: Tyler Davis'.

'Can I help you, sir?' asked the receptionist replacing the telephone.

'May I see Mr Tyler Davis please?'

'Who shall I say is calling?'

'Mr Mark Roman.'

'Do you have an appointment, Mr Roman?'

'No I haven't, but if Mr Davis could give me a few minutes of his time I would be most grateful.'

'Just take a seat for a moment, sir.'

The seat offered was a low, soft, leather-covered armchair—the kind, thought Roman, that I sink so far into that I need a block and tackle to get out again.

Pre-occupied with these thoughts Roman did not notice the approach over the deep pile carpet of a young man in his early thirties.

'Mr Roman?'

Roman clambered awkwardly out of his low-slung chair and turned to face the new arrival.

'Yes, I'm Mark Roman. You're Tyler Davis?'

'I am. If you'd like to step into my office I can give you a few minutes.'

As Roman followed Davis through the open-plan office he was aware of eyes following them. Roman was used to this—it had been happening to him for years—but he was aware that this time it was different. This time he was not just the object of the stares of the curious—'So that's what the voice looks like'. There was an added element of hostility towards the man who had discovered a corpse on their premises. Or perhaps it was more anxiety than hostility.

Davis led Roman to the senior executive office where the body had been found and closed the door behind them. He then surprised Roman by sitting down at the desk that the night before had been occupied by the corpse, and leaning back in the chair.

'I'm told this is where you found the body, Mr Roman?' He looked perfectly comfortable and relaxed.

'Yes, that's right.'

'This is actually my office. I had simply lent it to Salvador for the duration of his visit—and I didn't actually see the body here. The office had been cleaned up by the time I arrived. So you mustn't look surprised if I am working at my usual desk, despite what has happened.'

Davis presented a very cool, calm, phlegmatic exterior. An impression that was underlined by his well-cut, expensive business suit, his salon-cut hair, and his thin, faintly smiling face.

'What exactly is the purpose of your visit, Mr Roman?'

'May I ask you a few questions?'

'What about?'

'Well, mainly about Network Systems.'

'Very well Mr Roman. This is a very tight, efficient operation here and I'm happy to tell you about it. But only a few questions, since I can only spare you a few minutes.'

'How long has the company been in operation?'

'Here in Australia you mean?'

'Yes.'

'Around fifteen months.'

'Why was it established in Australia rather than Ecuador? Or anywhere else for that matter?'

'I don't really know the answer. Well, not in any detail I don't. I do know that there is little computer expertise in Ecuador so it was always going to be sensible to set up the computer centre outside of the headquarters country. As for the choice of Australia...well, we do have an international reputation for software generation here—perhaps that was it.'

'How well did you know Salvador Escobar?'

'This visit was the third time I had met him. The first was when he came to Australia to hire me as the foundation general manager of Network Systems, the second was when I flew to Ecuador twelve months ago for a briefing on the whole operation and the part that Network Systems would play in it, and the third was when he flew into Sydney two days ago.'

'Was this visit expected?'

'There was a fax on Monday saying he was on his way.'

'Fairly short notice, in other words?'

'Yes,' replied Davis, glancing at his watch.

Roman refused to take the hint. 'How did Simon Miller fit in here?'

'Very well. He was good at his job.'

'And socially: did he fit in well?'

'We are a very small operation here, Mr Roman. We have to get on with each other or get out.'

'Does that mean that there was friction between Simon and other staff members?'

'No real problems,' said the general manager stiffly.

'That implies there were, how shall I put it, occasional problems?'

'That's putting it too strongly. Simon was a surprisingly nervous young man. Insecure, I would have said. It made him behave as if he was very vain, very sensitive to any criticism of his work. But as I said, his work was good, so those situations rarely arose.'

'You would not have contemplated dismissing him?'

'Good grief no! There were no problems of that magnitude. And now, if you don't mind, Mr Roman, I have work that I must be getting on with.'

'Yes, of course. Thank you for your time, Mr Davis.'

Tyler Davis showed Roman to his office door, and closed it behind him.

Faces that had looked up when the door had opened and closed turned back to the work at their desks when they saw Roman looking back at them. All except one.

A tall, slim woman, with close-cropped blonde hair, dressed in an expensive business suit, rose from her desk and came towards him.

'Mr Roman?' she asked.

'Yes.'

'Pleased to meet you,' she said, extending a hand to shake. 'I'm Michelle Thomas, head of sales here at Network Systems. I understand that you personally stumbled across our little tragedy last night.'

'I found the body, if that's what you mean,' said Roman, reacting snappishly to the coy euphemism. 'Tell me, why is there a sales department in Network Systems? I thought this operation only developed software programs for Earthfast?'

'Yes, we do that. But once they are developed it makes good financial sense to market those software packages outside the parent company as well.'

'And how are sales going?'

'Slowly at first, but picking up now.'

'Did you know Salvador Escobar personally?'

'Yes,' she replied. 'I met him six months ago when I was flown to Ecuador for a briefing in the whole Earthfast operation.'

'And did you get on well with him?'

'Well enough. But if you want me to be brutally frank I'll tell you that he was too much like his father for my liking.'

'Now that interests me. Just exactly what do you mean by that?'

'I mean all this "goody goody" stuff. In sales there is not a lot of room for "niceness"; in sales you've got to go for the jugular, close the deal, without worrying about treading on the other fellow's toes.'

'Did you meet Raffael Escobar when you were in Ecuador?'

'Yes I did.'

'What was he like?'

'Very nice—in an overwhelming sort of way. Meeting Raffael Escobar is a bit like meeting the President of the United States or the Queen of England—very nice, but overwhelming. I suppose it's being descended from a thousand years of Spanish nobility that does it.'

'And what about Simon Miller—what do you think of him?'

'Simon is a nerd!' she snapped.

'I hate it when you use those Americanisms,' said a gravelly voice behind them.

Roman turned around to find himself facing a short,

squat man with ginger hair and a ginger beard.

'Mr Roman, this is our chief engineer, Paul Ferris,' said Michelle Thomas, making the necessary introductions, 'and, Paul, this is Mark Roman.'

'Yes, I'd know the voice even if I didn't know the face. Good afternoon, Mr Roman, a pleasure to meet you.'

'And the computer business is filled with Americanisms,' continued Michelle Thomas, 'so it's pointless complaining about one more.'

'Perhaps you meant that the remark was unfair, Mr Ferris?' suggested Roman.

'Oh, no. It's fair enough. Simon is a bit wimpish.'

'There you go,' said Thomas in a haughty voice, 'another Americanism.'

'All right, all right,' said Ferris flapping his hands in mock apology.

'Can I ask you both what it is about Simon that makes you describe him in this way?'

'Well, for a start, he's not here today,' snapped Thomas, her blue eyes blazing. 'The rest of us could make it but little Simon was too shaken by a death in the business to turn up.'

They don't yet know, thought Roman, that the dead man was Simon's long-estranged brother. Perhaps she'll regret those words when she is told of the relationship.

'I don't like to run someone down behind his back,' said Ferris, dropping his voice to a confidential tone, 'but truly, Simon is too full of himself. He's good at his work, but he imagines he is about seventeen times better than he is.'

'And that makes him sensitive to the mildest criticism,' added Thomas. 'He flies off the handle pretty easily.'

112

'And what makes him a wimp,' said the engineer, 'is that there is some kind of insecurity underlying it all.'

'He's over pampered, that's his trouble,' added the sales manager. 'That aunt of his, the one who brought him up, she pampers and protects him and fusses over him like he was five years old.'

'How do you know?'

'She came into the office once, I forget why,' replied Thomas, 'and you only needed to watch them for five minutes to see what the relationship between them was like. Mind you, Simon found her fussing over him in front of the whole office pretty embarrassing.'

'That's probably why he can't talk to women his own age,' said Ferris, scratching his ginger beard thoughtfully.

'No, that's where you're wrong Paul,' interrupted Thomas, 'Simon has got a thing going with our little receptionist.'

'Has he indeed!' said Ferris. 'The sly dog. I never suspected.'

'Just what is the relationship,' asked Roman, 'between Simon and the receptionist?'

'Her name's Naomi—Naomi Parker,' explained Thomas, 'and she's either Simon's girlfriend or his fiancée—I'm not sure which.'

'I see. Well, thank you both for your time,' said Roman. He shook them both by the hand and made his way across the office to the reception desk.

Naomi Parker was occupied typing a document and paid no attention to Roman, expecting him to walk straight past to the lifts. When she realised he was standing in front of her she looked up with a slightly startled look on her face.

'Can I. . .can I do something for you, Mr Roman?'

'I'd like to talk to you about Simon,' said Roman, dropping his voice half an octave, and speaking quietly and gently.

Naomi Parker looked to be twenty or twenty-one years of age, she had honey-blonde hair and green eyes and, Roman thought, a rather pale and uninteresting face.

'Yes...yes...I'll talk to you about Simon. Some of the others don't like him very much, but I'll tell you what he's really like. But not here, not now.'

'Where then? And when?' asked Roman.

'Tomorrow's Saturday,' said Naomi, scribbling on a piece of notepaper as she spoke, 'This is my phone number. Ring me at home tomorrow morning and we can arrange to meet somewhere.'

'Fine, I'll do that,' said Roman pocketing the note. 'Until tomorrow then.'

She smiled faintly in response, and Roman turned towards the lifts.

Anyone watching Roman eat his salad that night would have been struck by the stony, impassive look on his face. There was now so much to absorb and Roman was trying to take it all in. He was feeling that the only way he could understand this human drama was to, in his imagination, play all the different roles himself—to get inside the skins of each of the people involved.

After he'd loaded the dishwasher, he sprawled across the sofa to watch as much as he could of the evening's news and current affairs programs before heading off to the radio station.

With a cool drink in one hand and the remote control in the other, he flicked around all the news bulletins—Nine, Seven, Ten, ABC, SBS—and between the current affairs shows, catching slabs of Derryn

114

Hinch, Jana Wendt and Quentin Dempster.

At eight o'clock he turned off the set and headed off to work. He knew he should have gone earlier but this way he would avoid answering any more questions from curious colleagues about the murder.

On his show that night the talk-back callers, thankfully, kept away from the topic of murder and its punishment. During the day the appointment had been announced of a former cabinet minister to a highly paid administrative position in the state government, and this 'jobs for the boys' move provoked a number of outraged calls; and a proposal that there should be no mandatory retirement age, that people should be allowed to work for as long as they wanted to, was debated vigorously.

Then just after the eleven o'clock news a caller who identified himself as Gerard rang to air his personal sense of injury.

'This goes back some ten years, Mark,' he began, 'but I'll keep it as short as I can.'

'Yes, just give us the *Readers' Digest* condensed version, Gerard.'

'Right. As I say, it started ten years ago when my wife and I both went to work at the same place—we have no children. It's a small instrument making factory—I'm an instrument maker, and my wife worked in the office. The place had just been moved from Melbourne by the owner. He seemed like a really nice old bloke then.'

'You've changed your mind since?' asked Roman.

'Just wait till you've heard the rest of the story. Anyway, it's a small factory with only twenty-five employees. And the owner—I'd better not tell you his name, or the name of the factory, just in case I say something defamatory—the owner told us that he

115

intended to run the company for ten years and then retire. He also told us that, because he had no family and no heirs, when he retired he would give the ownership of the company to us, the employees.'

'Sounds very generous.'

'That's the way it sounded to us at the time too. So we have worked there for ten years.'

'And now he has reneged on his promise?'

'No! It's worse than that!'

'How could it be worse?'

'Let me tell you. A month ago he said the time had come to retire. Today he called us all together and announced that he had registered the company as a limited liability company with one thousand fully paid up shares, and these shares he proceeded to give to the staff. Twenty-five employees I said, right?'

'I remember.'

'And he gave everyone forty shares each.'

'That works out mathematically—twenty-five times forty equals one thousand. That sounds fair.'

'But it's not! It's not fair at all!'

'I don't understand.'

'You see, my wife and I and eight others have been there for the whole ten years. But there are others who have been there for a much shorter time than us. There are some who have been there for four, five or six years, and there's one young man who's only been there three months. Yet everyone got the same—forty shares!'

'What you mean is, you weren't rewarded for your length of service?'

'That's right! That's right! That's exactly right! How dare that old bloke—who'd been pretending he was such a fair old bloke—how dare he—'

'You mean the owner?'

116

'Yes, the owner. How dare he give the same number of shares to someone who's only been there three months as he's given me and my wife who've been there for ten whole years! It stinks! It really stinks! So what can I do about it, Mark? I must have some recourse.'

'I doubt that you have any legal recourse over what is, after all, a gift.'

'What I want, Mark, is justice! If our legal system can't give me justice in this matter then there must be something seriously wrong!'

'Just stop and think for a moment, Gerard,' said Roman, trying to work out how he was going to tackle this one.

'I have been thinking, Mark. That's all I've done all day is think about this, and about how unfair it is. And it's all my wife and I have talked about since we got home from work today.'

'What I mean is, stand back and try to get this into some sort of perspective.'

'Waddya mean?'

'I mean the owner didn't *have* to give the company to his employees, did he? I mean, he could have looked for a buyer and *sold* the company, couldn't he?'

'Wouldn't have been easy, not with a recession on.'

'But he could have, couldn't he?'

'If he'd done that he would have broken his promise—the one he made ten years ago.'

'Yes, but my point is that he never needed to make that promise in the first place, did he?'

'Well, no one *forced* him to make it. It was his own idea.'

'Exactly.'

'I don't follow.' Gerard was sounding puzzled.

'The owner was simply being generous when he

117

made the promise ten years ago, and today he has been exactly as generous to you, your wife and the other ten-year employees as he promised to be then. That's true, isn't it?'

'Yes, that's true. . . but. . . if everyone had stayed on for the whole ten years it wouldn't have mattered. But some people have left and others have joined, and they are not entitled to what we are entitled to.'

'Look,' said Roman, 'I can understand how you feel, but the truth is that you are not *entitled* to *anything*. Whatever you get, it is an act of pure generosity on the part of the owner. How then can you object to him being generous to other people?'

'But I can! And I do! If he wants to be generous, then he has to be generous absolutely fairly!'

'Says who? Who is making these rules about generosity? Did the owner make these rules when he first announced his intention ten years ago?'

'No. Back then he just said the ownership of the company would be divided equally between the employees.'

'And that's what he has now done, isn't it?'

'But some employees have contributed less than others—less time working at the plant is what I mean.'

'That's where you're wrong Gerard. None of you has contributed *anything* towards this handout of shares.'

'If you're saying, Mark, that my wife and I have just been loafing for the past ten years. . .'

'No! Don't get me wrong, Gerard. That's not what I'm saying at all. But all the hard work you have done for the past ten years you have been *paid* for, haven't you? You collected your pay packet each week, didn't you?'

'Yes, of course.'

118

'That was your reward for working for ten years: ten years of pay packets. This gift of shares has nothing to do with rewards or entitlements. It is a gift to which no one, not you, not your wife, not the newer workers, not anyone, is *entitled* to. It's just something you are being given freely as a gift.'

Gerard went away still grumbling and complaining.

Two calls later, a woman named Grace rang to make her own comment about Gerard's complaint. 'He's just jealous because his boss is generous, that's all,' she said.

'I'm afraid you're right,' said Roman. 'But I couldn't seem to get that through to him.'

'I heard that, and he was so blinkered I was getting quite angry with him. He didn't seem to understand the nature of generosity.'

'Exactly right.' said Roman. 'In fact since he rang I have been trying to think of the word that summed up the nature of generosity, and when I saw your name on the computer screen I remembered. It was "grace", Grace.' Roman gave a self-indulgent chuckle. 'It's a technical word—a theological word, actually.'

'My mother always told me that "grace" means "beauty and elegance".'

'Well, she wasn't wrong. That is *one* of the meanings of "grace" that you'll find in the dictionary. But in theological terms, it means—you'll also find this in the dictionary—the "freely given unmerited favour and love of God". Someone has summed it up by saying that "grace", in this sense, means "surprising generosity". And that's probably putting it mildly: "astonishing generosity", or "mind-blowing generosity", or "amazing generosity" would be better.'

'Like in that song,' said Grace, the caller.

'What song?'

119

' "Amazing Grace".'

Roman laughed. 'You're pretty amazing yourself, Grace. But yes, that's the point. Poor old Gerard is being treated with amazing, surprising generosity by the company owner and he is so obsessed with what other people are getting that he can't see it. Very sad really.'

Gerard's story and Grace's response provoked enough calls to keep the board full until midnight.

As soon as the show was over Roman hurried home to yet another cold shower.

By one o'clock in the morning he was exhausted and ready to flop into bed.

As he lay there on his hot mattress trying to fall asleep, Roman had a feeling that there was something that was almost within his grasp...but not quite. Something that should have come together for him out of the events of the day. And, just as sleep was capturing him, he thought he had it.

But when the morning came, it was gone again.

Chapter 7

Roman woke up in a lather of sweat, and with a heavy feeling that told him he hadn't slept well. At least, not well enough.

It was Saturday and he lay across the tangle of sheets that was his bed, reluctant to rise and begin the day.

Eventually, by sheer will-power, he forced himself out of bed and, like clockwork, went through his usual morning routine: showered, shaved, dressed, set the percolator going, and walked up to the Kirribilli shops to buy hot bread rolls and the morning paper.

As he ate, Roman leafed through the thick Saturday edition of the *Telegraph-Mirror*. The murder, he discovered, had been relegated to page three, but it managed to dominate that page with the news that police had revealed the identity of the victim.

The report didn't tell him a thing that he didn't already know. In a side-bar story, however, he did find some new and interesting information. The boxed column told him that the victim's father, the famous

Raffael Escobar, had already left Ecuador to fly to Australia and was expected to arrive at Sydney Airport tomorrow afternoon.

Roman picked up the telephone, dialled the number of his own radio station, and asked for the newsroom.

The phone was answered with an abrupt 'News here'. Roman recognised the voice.

'Rob, it's Mark Roman here. Have you got a minute?'

'Sure.'

'According to this morning's paper, Raffael Escobar is flying into Sydney tomorrow: can you check on when he's due for me please?'

'Raffael Escobar? That's the father of the dead bloke you found, isn't it?'

'That's right.'

'Hang on, I'll just pull up the AAP diary on the computer.'

The handpiece must have been set down on the desk next to the keyboard because Roman could hear the click of the keys as Rob went into 'wires all' on the newsroom computer and then entered the instruction 'find diary–sunday'. A moment later he was back on the phone.

'I've got it in front of me now, Mark. Just hang on while I scroll through. Do you know if he's due morning or afternoon?'

'Afternoon.'

'This won't take long, I'll just scroll through. Ah, here we are. Raffael Escobar is arriving on a Continental flight via Hawaii at 3.45 pm.'

'Thanks for that, Rob. I owe you one.'

'No problems, Mark. Catch you later.'

As he replaced his telephone Roman made up his mind that he would be at the airport tomorrow afternoon to meet the plane. He wasn't sure that he wanted to speak to Escobar, in fact he thought it unlikely that he'd get a chance. But he did want to see the man. He wanted to get close enough to see the man's face. Somehow he had a feeling that this whole drama revolved around the personality of Raffael Escobar.

Roman tidied up his kitchen and then, with some reluctance, tackled his regular Saturday morning housekeeping chores; he vacuumed, and swept, and dusted, and mopped the kitchen and bathroom floors.

The work done he sat down for his second cup of coffee for the day when he remembered a phone call he had to make. The scrap of paper containing the telephone number was in the pocket of yesterday's shirt, and had to be retrieved from the dirty clothes basket.

He managed to read the number on the crumpled slip and dialled it.

'Hello?' It was an older, male voice that answered.

'May I speak to Naomi Parker, please?'

'Who shall I say is calling?'

'Mark Roman.'

'Oh, so it is! I thought I recognised the voice. Hold the line please, Mr Roman.'

For a minute or so Roman could hear distant voices in the background, but he was unable to distinguish any of the words. The phone at the other end was picked up again.

'Hello? Mr Roman?'

'Is that you, Naomi?'

'Yes it is.'

'Can we get together sometime today to have a chat about Simon?'

There was a long silence on the line.

'You did promise to talk to me today,' said Roman, 'and it's important that I get to see the full picture, the full truth.'

'All right then.'

'When and where?'

'I live with my parents at Artarmon. Can you come here?'

'Easily. What time?'

'How would half past eleven do?'

'That'd be fine. Give me the address.'

Naomi gave Roman an address in Kitchener Road, Artarmon and rang off.

Checking his watch, Roman saw that he just had time to get his other regular Saturday morning chore of shopping out of the way before he left for Artarmon.

At Shoppingworld in Berry Street, North Sydney, he hurried through his purchases and at the checkout made his usual joke about having balanced his purchases among the five food groups—tinned, frozen, dried, junk, and instant.

When his groceries had been unpacked into the kitchen cupboards, there were still a few minutes to spare, and Roman decided to make another phone call before leaving for Artarmon.

'Hello?'

'Is that you, Liz? It's Mark here—Mark Roman.'

'Oh, Mark. It's nice to hear your voice again.'

'How's it going? Has Simon sat down and had a long talk to you and Bertram yet?'

'No, he's still not talking to us, Mark. We can hardly get a word out of him.'

'Well, don't let it worry you. He'll talk to you when he's good and ready.'

'But it does worry me, Mark. I can't help worrying about it.'

'That's understandable. I just wish there was more that I could say to reassure you.'

'Why don't you come to afternoon tea this afternoon, Mark?'

'Well. . . I don't know. . .'

'Bertram and I would like that. And Simon might agree to join us. With you there he might even open up and start talking.'

'I don't know so much about that.'

'And anyway, Bertram and I would like to hear about your investigation, and what you've discovered so far.'

Roman didn't really want to talk about what he had, or hadn't learnt so far. He was still at a stage where he wanted to absorb information and facts and feelings rather than give them out. But, driven by the feeling that there was more to learn from the Miller household, he agreed.

'All right—afternoon tea then. What time?'

'Three o'clock. How would that be?'

'Fine. I'll see you at three then.'

Roman dropped the phone back onto its cradle trying to work out just what it was about Liz's voice that he found so unusual. Perhaps, he thought, it was the combination of opposites: a quavering insecurity, but underneath a certainty or determination that was as hard as iron.

Roman shrugged off the problem, locked up the apartment, and went back down to his car.

Kitchener Road, Artarmon, turned out to be a street of almost identical suburban bungalows. They were all older style homes, of cavity-brick construction, with terracotta tiled roofs. The street was quiet and deserted: baked into immobility by the blazing heat of an unseasonable December.

Blinds and curtains were drawn to keep the heat out of the houses, and those homes that had incongruous aluminium awnings fitted to the front windows had those awnings fully extended against the sun. Roman found the number he was looking for in the middle of the street, and parked the Volvo in the shade of a jacaranda tree that was still a blaze of purple.

Having pressed the door-bell Roman waited on the front step, feeling the heat beating back from the brick walls. He didn't have to wait long. It was Naomi herself who opened the door.

'Come in, Mr Roman. This way,' she said, and led him down a dim hallway into a back living area that was clearly an addition to the original house. It had a lower ceiling, light coloured walls, concealed lighting, and a back wall consisting entirely of sliding glass doors which opened onto a small but beautifully maintained backyard garden.

'Who's the gardener?' asked Roman.

'That's Mum's garden,' said Naomi with little pride or interest.

In the middle of the garden, on a pocket-handkerchief piece of lawn, a rotary sprinkler was running. The sight reminded Roman of his own childhood, and of running through the sprinkler on hot days. He had grown up before swimming pools became commonplace in Sydney and children found relief during heatwaves from the lawn sprinkler and the garden hose.

His thoughts were interrupted by the arrival of a middle-aged couple through an archway that Roman guessed would lead to a modern kitchen—another part of the extension to the original house.

'Mr Roman,' said Naomi, 'this is my mum and dad.'

'How do you do, Mr Roman? I'm Ted and this is Joan,' said Naomi's father, performing the introductions.

'I've been making up a jug of iced tea for the family, Mr Roman,' said Joan. 'Would you like a glass?'

'That sounds very refreshing, thank you. And please call me Mark.'

Joan returned to the kitchen and soon the clinking of glassware could be heard. Ted let himself out through the sliding glass doors, and a moment later Roman saw him turn off the sprinkler, adjust its position, and turn it back on again.

'Take a seat please, Mr Roman,' said Naomi, while this was going on.

Roman lowered himself into an over-padded leather armchair. 'Thank you for agreeing to talk to me Naomi,' he said.

'I do want you to know what Simon is really like,' she replied, not looking him in the eyes, but staring down at her fingers as she spoke, 'and those other people at Network Systems don't like him.'

'Why don't they like him?'

'Because they don't know him as well as I do—'

'Here we are then.' Naomi's mother was back with four tall glasses of iced tea on a tray, each with several ice cubes and a slice of lemon floating on top.

Ted returned from the garden and took his glass just as Roman and Naomi were being served. 'Well, if you'll excuse me, Mr Roman, I'll take this out to the shed—I've got some work to do.'

'Yes, of course.'

'And I have to keep working on lunch,' said Joan making her way back to the kitchen.

'Your parents are very tactful,' said Roman, turning to Naomi.

'What do you mean?'

'Just that it might be easier for you to talk honestly about Simon if they are not here.'

'I had no intention of saying anything dishonest,' she replied with a sullen pout.

'No, of course not,' muttered Roman. 'Now, just how long have you known Simon?'

'Ever since I started work at Network Systems.'

'Which is how long?'

'About eight months.'

'And when did you two start becoming friends?'

'It's hard to say. Simon used to stop and talk to me whenever he walked past the reception desk. And then I noticed that he was walking past my desk rather more often than he really needed to. And that's when I thought he might really like me.'

'And did you like him?'

'Well, I never had a boyfriend, all the way through high school and then business college. I was always the shy one in the group.'

'What you're saying is that Simon was the first young man to really take an interest in you?'

'Hhmmm,' was her only reply, and she looked back down at her fingers again.

'So that was how it started. How did the relationship develop?'

'We started going to lunch together. In fact, our lunch hours were the times when we really got to know one another.'

'The sales manager at your office—what's her name?'

'That's Michelle Thomas.'

'That's right. She said she was unclear about whether you were Simon's girlfriend, or his fiancée: which is it?'

128

'Simon and I are engaged to be married,' said Naomi, throwing her head back.

'But. . .?' prompted Roman. 'There's more to it than that, isn't there?'

'It's just that his aunt and uncle don't know yet.'

'Do your parents know?'

'Oh, yes! Mum and Dad have met Simon, and they like him. They know all about it.'

'Then why not Simon's aunt and uncle?'

'Simon said his aunt would be upset, and that he'd have to break it to her gently.'

'Have you met them yet? Simon's aunt and uncle I mean?'

'No, not yet. Simon was going to arrange for me to meet them soon, but then this terrible business has happened, and that will throw our plans out of gear I have no doubt.'

'Did Simon's aunt even know that he was going out with you?'

Naomi looked back down at her fingers, which were twisting around one another.

'Had Simon told them?' persisted Roman.

'I don't think so,' said Naomi quietly.

'Did he explain why?'

'He told me about his mother being killed when he was young, and about his aunt escaping with him to Australia. He said that because of that she, Aunt Liz, was over-protective. And because she had been so good to him, Simon wanted to be careful not to hurt her.'

'I see.'

'I did see Simon's Aunt Liz once, when she called in to the office to see him about something. But I didn't speak to her.'

'Simon didn't take the opportunity to introduce you?'

'No.'

'You said you wanted me to understand what Simon is really like—well, what is he really like?'

'He means well,' said Naomi speaking rapidly and passionately. 'He's gentle really, and his intentions are very good. He finds it hard to cope with criticism, I think because his Aunt Liz has such high expectations of him. But if he flies off the handle he always regrets it afterwards. He said to me a week ago that he was going to turn over a new leaf, exercise more self discipline, and not let these other people in the office get under his skin again.'

'I see,' said Roman thoughtfully.

Just then Naomi's mother came bustling back in through the archway leading to the kitchen.

'Lunch is almost ready,' she said. 'Will you stay and eat with us, Mr Roman?'

'No. It's kind of you to offer, but I really must be going.'

Roman saw Naomi's quick glance of appreciation as he rejected the invitation. She saw him to the front door.

'Thanks for your help, Naomi.'

'Thank you for being so understanding,' said the young woman. 'Simon's going to be all right, isn't he?'

'I'm sure he is,' said Roman warmly, expressing a confidence he did not feel.

From Kitchener Road, Roman drove down to the Artarmon shopping centre confident that there he could satisfy a desire that had been niggling at him since the heatwave started. It was illogical he knew, but Roman had a craving for old-fashioned fish and chips. For some reason he always associated fish and chips with hot weather. Perhaps because when he was a child Roman's parents had bought fish and chips on holidays and rarely at other times. And holidays were always in the summer and on the beach.

Roman found a shop that sold fish and chips in the little Artarmon shopping centre. Nowadays his take-away serving was wrapped in white butcher's paper, not newspaper, as it had been in his childhood, and a sign above the deep frying vats announced that only 'cholesterol free vegetable oils' were used in cooking.

But after he had indulged himself in the greasy feast, he was hot again, and his stomach felt uncomfortably full, and he wished he had resisted the craving.

He cleaned up the kitchen and turned on the exhaust fan to get rid of the greasy smell, then dug through his collection of CDs and came up with *Buddy Holly's Greatest Hits*. As the music began to play, Roman told himself that he would never fully escape his disc-jockey past. And he wasn't sure that he wanted to.

He stripped off his outer clothing, turned on the ceiling fan, and lay down on the sofa to listen. But within minutes, he fell into a weary sleep.

When he woke up he felt confused and disoriented. What time was it? What was he supposed to be doing this afternoon?

Roman struggled to the bathroom, splashed cold water on his face, and gathered his thoughts. That's right, afternoon tea with the Millers. . . three o'clock. Where was his watch? Oh good, it was only two-thirty, plenty of time.

At Wollstonecraft he found the same shady peppercorn tree to prop the Volvo under. But this time, as he turned off the engine and opened the car door, his ears were pierced by a skull-splitting sound. The peppercorn tree was full of cicadas, all of them a dull

131

green colour barely visible against the leaves and branches—'Greengrocers' he had called them when he was a child.

He stood there for a moment remembering the velvet bodies, the cellophane wings, and the didgeridoo drone of the captive cicadas that he and his friends had kept in shoe boxes, then locked the car behind him and strode purposefully towards the rambling old two-storey house.

The doorbell was answered, after some delay, by Liz. 'Come in, Mark, come in,' she said, with an expression on her face that said 'I'm struggling to be cheerful and a good hostess but I'm finding it hard'.

They exchanged courtesies as Roman followed Liz down the dark—and delightfully cool—hallway to the small sitting room in which he had been entertained on his first visit.

'Bertram is out the back somewhere,' said Liz. 'I'll tell him to go and find Simon while I put on the kettle. You take a seat and make yourself at home, Mark. We shouldn't keep you long.'

Left on his own and unable to sit still, perhaps because he had only recently awoken from sleep, Roman paced restlessly around the room looking first at the photographs—almost all were of the two sisters, Liz and Simon's mother Peggy.

A series of black-and-white photographs in large, clumsy, old fashioned frames showed the two girls side by side in school uniforms, in swimming costumes, in Girl Guides uniforms and, more grown up, in nurses' uniforms. Then there were wedding photos of Liz and Bertram, but significantly missing were Peggy's wedding photos. Perhaps, thought Roman, because Peggy's marriage to Raffael Escobar had been such a distressing event for Liz.

132

Having exhausted the photographs he began to examine the furniture. There were several polished walnut bookcases with glass doors. Roman examined one of them with envy. It was exactly what he would like to store all his golf books.

At the end of the room was an old fashioned roll-top desk. Roman tried pushing up the top and discovered it was unlocked. Feeling a little like a schoolboy exploring the headmaster's study, he pushed the roll-top all the way up and looked at the mess of papers scattered on the narrow surface of the desk.

After a furtive glance over his shoulder, Roman began to examine these papers. He knew he was going beyond the bounds of decency, but he could not control his need to understand, to get inside the skins of these people.

The bills were of the most ordinary household kind and told him nothing. So he turned his attention to the drawers. In the left-hand drawer he came across a thick wad of papers that were stamped and endorsed like some sort of legal documents. It took him several moments to realise just what they were: share certificates. Roman leafed through the pile reading the company names. Although his knowledge of finance was only slight he recognised most of the names as belonging to what finance reporters call 'blue chip' companies.

Then he tried the right-hand drawer. There were more household bills on top, but underneath he found a whole series of letters from a major firm of stock-brokers. He read a few paragraphs here and there. The stock transactions they referred to seemed to his untrained eye to be quite large ones.

This hardly fitted with what Liz had said about

scrimping and saving to get Simon through university. But then, Roman told himself, lots of people liked to 'cry poor' when they are far from it, so perhaps he shouldn't be surprised...

A rattle in the hallway made Roman start guiltily. He hurriedly closed the drawer and the roll-top and stepped back towards the middle of the room.

Liz came in carrying a tea tray, followed by Bertram still wearing his almost colourless old cardigan—despite the weather.

'Bertram says that Simon is out in the backyard, taking a little fresh air. Apparently he doesn't want any afternoon tea. But perhaps you can go and talk to him there after you've had yours.'

'Yes,' said Roman. 'Why not?'

'Now tell us,' said Liz as she poured, 'just what you've been doing to help Simon, and what you have found out so far.'

Roman accepted a cup of tea, added milk and sugar, refused the offer of a biscuit, and leaned back in the sofa to tell them his story. He gave them only a potted summary of events and he tactfully omitted the character analysis of Simon offered by Michelle Thomas and Paul Ferris at Network Systems. He also left out all references to Naomi Parker. That, he decided, was up to Simon to tell his aunt.

Those omissions left his narrative rather short, so Roman padded it out by giving a very full account of his meeting with Detective Sergeant Bob Lineham. This interested Liz, and she homed in at once on the question of whether or not Simon was a suspect.

'Well,' said Roman carefully, 'He was the last to see the deceased alive—'

'Apart from the murderer!' interposed Liz quickly.

'—Yes, apart from the murderer. And the murder

134

weapon was a letter-pener that normally sat on his desk.'

'Doesn't mean a thing!' said Liz with certainty.

'It might mean that the murderer was deliberately trying to frame Simon,' suggested Roman.

'Not necessarily,' insisted Liz. 'How would the murderer know whose desk he was picking up the murder weapon from? No, I'm quite convinced that was simply a matter of convenience. The murderer was looking for a weapon and Simon's letter-pener lay close to hand.'

'You are in all probability right,' said Roman. 'The question is whether or not the police see it that way.'

'That's what worries me,' said Liz quietly, her confidence quickly evaporating. 'You said it was all a matter of motive, in your discussion with that detective didn't you?'

'With Bob Lineham? Yes, that's right. They are not going to be interested in proceeding against Simon unless they have a clear and strong motive—something that justifies murder.'

'And there isn't one, is there?'

'Well, I've been thinking about that. What about inheritance?'

'What do you mean?' asked Liz sharply.

'It must have occurred to you, Liz,' said Roman, 'that Raffael Escobar is a very wealthy man who has—or rather *had*—only two heirs: Simon and the dead man.'

'For a start we don't know if that man still has Simon in his will,' replied Liz. 'When Bertram and I escaped to Australia with young Simon, and refused to hand him over to that man, he may well have cut Simon out of the will altogether.'

'Yes, he may. And that is no doubt something the

Australian police will make inquiries about.'

'But even if Simon is still in the will, killing that Salvador person gives him no immediate benefit. That man is not about to die I take it?'

'You mean Raffael Escobar? No, to the best of my knowledge he is in fine health.'

'There! You see. Simon would have to wait twenty or thirty years to gain any benefit from this murder, and what sort of a motive is that?'

'Not a very strong one, I agreed.'

'What will the police do next, Mark?'

'I really have no idea, Liz. We'll just have to wait and see.'

'And you'll keep in touch with them, won't you?'

'Certainly.'

'And look after Simon's interests. He does need looking after you know. If he became upset during a police interview he could be quite rude to them, and that would create entirely the wrong impression. I mean, fundamentally he's a very nice boy, Simon. I'm very proud of him. He is gentle and considerate and well intentioned. But sometimes he gets a bit carried away.'

'And that can be unfortunate. Yes, I take your point entirely, Liz. Well, I will certainly continue with my inquiries, whether they will produce any results or not is a question I cannot answer at this stage.'

'Thank you, Mark.' Liz accompanied these words by reaching out and, to Roman's great embarrassment, patting his hand, almost as a maternal display of approval.

Roman rose to his feet. 'Why don't I wander out into the backyard and see if Simon feels like a chat? Nice to have seen you again, Bertram,' he added.

Bertram, slouched unseeingly in his lounge chair

had contributed not a word to the conversation. 'Huh? Hmmm? Oh, yes,' said the old man, rousing himself from his drowsy introspection.

'Which way to the backyard?' asked Roman.

'Straight down the hall, turn left, and through the screen door,' replied Liz.

Roman followed the directions and found himself blinking into the blaze of sunlight streaming through an insect-screen security door that looked very new compared to the rest of this old house.

On the other side of the screen door was a sprawling lawn fringed with low shrubs and the occasional gum tree. As his eyes adjusted to the light, Roman recognised Simon slouched on a garden seat in the speckled shade of a spindly eucalypt up near the back fence.

Roman sat down beside him. 'How are you today, Simon?' he asked gently.

There was no response from the sullen young man on the garden seat.

Roman sat down beside him. 'How are you today, Simon' he asked gently.

'Fine thanks,' was the brisk dismissive reply.

'You haven't spoken to your aunt or uncle yet?'

'Not yet.'

'When will you?'

'I'm thinking about it.'

'You said yesterday that there were some things you needed to think through, and some decisions you had to make. Have you made them yet?'

'Not yet,' mumbled Simon, who then turned and faced Roman directly. 'I'm out here getting some fresh air and clearing my head. I was hoping for some privacy.'

'It's a bit hot to be sitting out of doors, isn't it?'

'It's worse in there,' said Simon, nodding towards the house.

'By the way, have you decided to tell Liz and Bertram about Naomi yet?'

Simon glanced up, a look of sheer panic in his eyes. 'What about Naomi?' he said, his chin raised in defiant challenge.

'She tells me you're engaged,' said Roman softly.

Simon swore under his breath.

'Don't worry, I won't tell anyone I shouldn't tell. Especially I won't be telling your aunt and uncle. That's your business.'

A wave of relief passed over Simon's face. 'Thanks. You're not a bad bloke, Mr Roman. I apologise for being so snappy just now—and the last time we spoke. But you'll understand that there's a lot . . .' he left the sentence unfinished.

'I understand.'

Simon stood up and started walking slowly across the lawn, apparently oblivious to the furnace-like sun beating down upon him.

Roman leaped up and walked beside him. 'Do you know that your father is arriving tomorrow?'

'Yeah. I saw it in the paper,' replied the younger man.

As they reached the back wall of the house, Roman turned to say, 'If there's anything I can do . . .', but he was halted in his tracks by the look of pain that clouded the young man's face.

Suddenly, with no warning at all, Simon kicked savagely at the garbage bin near the back door snarling, 'Why the hell did all this have to happen!'

The bin clattered across a cement path, spilling its contents.

Simon turned to look at Roman, an embarrassed

and foolish expression on his face. 'Sorry,' he said lamely. 'I'm just...just carrying so much at the moment...'

'Never mind,' said Roman. 'Just give me a hand to clear up this mess.'

As he spoke he bent over and started shovelling milk cartons, orange juice cartons, cigarette cartons, cabbage leaves and parcels of tea leaves back into the garbage bin.

'Here, let me do that,' said Simon. 'I'll look after this. You're a visitor, and it's my mess anyway.'

As Simon bent down and took over the cleaning up, Roman straightened up. For a moment Roman stood there, looking down at the young man, trying to imagine what it would be like, at that very moment, to inhabit his skin, to feel his feelings, to think his thoughts.

'Just remember, if there's anything, anytime, just give me a call.'

'Sure,' said Simon, without looking up from his task.

Roman took his leave of Liz and Bertram, and walked back out to the Volvo and the deafening cacophony of cicadas. So pre-occupied was he that he was almost unaware of them.

As he settled into the driver's seat Roman muttered to himself, 'Now that's interesting—very interesting indeed.'

Chapter 8

That night Roman decided that he was in the mood for steak, but not in the mood to cook. So he drove to the Black Stump at North Sydney, for a scotch fillet, well barbecued, with a side salad.

He took his Bible with him so that he could check over the passage he was due to read at Carols by Candlelight a little later in the evening, and sat quietly in his car for ten minutes thinking over the day's events, before driving to the oval.

It was filled with family groups sitting on rugs on the grass. Roman thought of the little family he had lost and a pang of emptiness shot through his chest.

The Carols program ran very smoothly. Hugh Marsden, Roman knew from experience, was very good at organising and running such events. All the well known, and well loved, Christmas carols were sung in that warm, still evening air—a long way from the wintry northern hemisphere Christmases for which they'd been written.

The carols were interspersed with solo items as well

as Bible readings. Roman's short, three-point introduction, and then the reading itself, seemed to go well.

Hugh had included one or two songs which were, strictly speaking, not carols but fitted the theme of the evening and were well enough known to fit into the community singing mode. At about half-past eight, just as it was getting dark enough to start lighting the candles, Roman realised that the song they were to sing next was 'Amazing Grace'.

As they sang the words his thoughts went back to the call of the night before on his radio show and to the whole question of God's 'surprising generosity' to frail and faulty human beings.

Amazing grace how sweet the sound,
That saved a wretch like me.
I once was lost but now I'm found,
Was blind but now I see.

Roman found himself, as always, deeply moved by the words. And, as he sang, his thoughts drifted back to the murder of Salvador Escobar and the amazing lack of grace with which human beings so often treat each other in this grim benighted world.

Twas grace that taught my heart to fear,
And grace my fears relieved.
How precious did that grace appear,
The hour I first believed.

The thing that puzzled Roman was the total lack of interest that so many people displayed in God's generosity. It was almost a matter of pride in not being beholden to anyone—not even to God!

141

When we've been there ten thousand years,
Bright shining as the sun,
We've no less days to sing God's praise,
Than when we'd first begun.

The evening came to an early close—many of the family groups included very young children—and Roman made his way home.

A cup of coffee, followed by a glass of port, did nothing to overcome his restless, unsettled feeling. Quite often on a Saturday night Roman went to a movie but, on this particular Saturday, Carols by Candlelight had ended too late for that. He checked out the television program guide and found nothing that appealed to him.

Some twenty minutes later, he was still pacing up and down the short distance of his living room carpet and he knew he had to find some way to make himself sit down, relax, and forget about the Escobar murder case.

In the cabinet underneath his television set and video recorder he kept a collection of movies: an impressive, but incomplete, set of John Wayne classics. He browsed amongst them for some minutes and settled for one of the longest and best—John Ford's *The Searchers*. This would block unwanted thoughts from his mind for a couple of hours at least.

He loaded the machine, pressed the button, and settled back on the sofa. He could feel the tension start to drain out of his body as soon as the familiar titles appeared on the screen.

One hundred and nineteen minutes later Roman hit the re-wind button satisfied to let his mind dwell on the intricate ambiguities of John Ford's film rather than on the nagging problem of who killed Salvador Escobar and why.

142

While he was still in that slightly hypnotic state Roman changed into his pyjamas, turned off the lights and went to bed.

The next morning he woke early, or, at least, early for a habitual shift-worker like himself. Roman arose feeling refreshed and invigorated, and when he pulled back the bedroom curtains and opened the windows he discovered why. There was a breeze blowing, a fresh and cooling southerly breeze. The five-day heatwave was over. Roman opened the windows wide and let the brisk southerly whip into the apartment. Could he really smell the salt tang of the Pacific Ocean on that breeze, or was he only imagining it?·

Somehow the breeze was blowing away the fog that had filled his head for the last forty-eight hours. He showered, shaved, and dressed feeling sharper and clearer than he had for days.

Sunday brought its own regular routine. This always started with washing. Roman's 'laundry' was nothing more than a cupboard in one corner of his bathroom. When the slatted wooden door of this cupboard was opened it revealed a front-opening automatic washing machine sitting on the floor, and, fixed to the wall above it, a clothes drier. Roman loaded the washing machine with bedlinen and everything from the dirty-clothes basket, added soap powder, and set its automatic cycle running.

Before leaving he locked all the windows open with a burglar-proof 20 cm gap, then came the second part of the Sunday routine: getting the car washed. Because it spent so much time parked in the open, Roman made a point of washing it every week. Every Sunday morning without fail he drove to Neutral Bay and put the old green Volvo through the car-wash.

The staff provided him with a free cup of coffee,

as always, and he bought a newspaper, the *Sunday Telegraph*, there. While his car was being pulled through the sprays and spinning brushes he opened the paper and turned first, as he always did, to the radio column. The columnist had re-told the story of his finding the murdered corpse and added some details about the discussion this had provoked on his show. Roman was pleased to see that she had illustrated this item with a more recent publicity photo of himself.

From the car-wash Roman drove to the Cremorne delicatessen where he always ate his Sunday breakfast. This particular Sunday morning he ate bagels with smoked salmon and cottage cheese while he read slowly through the Sunday paper spread out on the table in front of him.

After this light meal—more of a brunch than a breakfast—he went home to the laborious task of putting the washing through the drier. By the time that was done it was time to drive to the rectory to have lunch with Hugh and Jill Marsden.

'I thought today would be too hot for anything but a salad,' said Jill as she opened the front door. 'And now this southerly change has blown up and cooled us all down.'

'It's not all that cool,' said Roman. 'Just comfortably cooler—salad will be fine, Jill, there's no need to make excuses.'

And, in fact, Jill's 'salad' turned out to be a superb selection: tossed garden salad, coleslaw, rice salad, seafood salad, potato salad and more. After the children had been served and settled down, Roman piled his own plate high.

'Tell me about this murder you've got mixed up in,' said Hugh as they ate. 'Have you drawn any conclusions?'

144

'I never draw conclusions,' replied Roman.

'But you must have some thoughts on it,' insisted Jill.

'The thought that is pre-occupying me at the moment,' replied Roman, 'is the nagging feeling that I have missed the most important element.'

'Which is?' asked Hugh.

'The character of the victim. I feel that to know the identity of the murderer I must know the victim well. And so far the victim is the most elusive of all the characters in this whole drama.'

'This is Salvador Escobar that you're talking about?'

'That's right.'

'So, what do you know about him so far?'

'I know that he is—or was—a wealthy young man. It appears fairly obvious that his father trusted him with certain managerial responsibilities; so, assuming that his father is intelligent, and we know he is, we can further conclude that Salvador was worthy of carrying these responsibilities.'

'Was he well educated?'

'That is something that I have not inquired into. But I am prepared to assume that he was. Certainly his father before him had been, and, to be trusted with managerial tasks by such a father, my guess is that he would have been well educated himself.'

'What kind of a person was he?'

'Ah, there Hugh you have put your finger on my problem. The answer is: I really don't know. One person I spoke to, a person who had met him, complained that he was "too much like his father".'

'And what did that mean?'

'I never found out exactly, beyond vague references to being too nice, too goody-goody—to be true, I suppose.'

'It always strikes me as odd,' said Hugh, 'when people object to goodness.'

'Yes, it is odd. But it's not unusual. It's a complaint that I get from time to time on the talk-back.'

'So, assuming that report is correct,' interposed Jill, 'and the victim, this Salvador Escobar, was a good man, a nice man, even a likeable man, what does that tell you about the murderer?'

'What it should do is make me ask the right questions,' replied Roman.

'What questions?'

'Such as: What kind of murderer does a good man, a genuinely good man, attract? Who can be harmed by the actions of a good man? Who can benefit from the death of a good man?'

'And what are the answers to those questions?'

'I know none of the answers, I only know that asking the right questions is half the battle.'

After lunch, Roman, Hugh and Jill sat around and talked in the lengthy, rambling, often jokey way that friends talk after a meal, while Hugh and Jill's young daughters played happily around their feet. Visits to Hugh and Jill, and his other married friends, were important to Roman—they gave him a taste of the domestic life he had been denied.

'Tell me something, Mark,' said Jill, as the three of them were dawdling over coffee.

'Anything,' said Roman expansively, feeling heavy and relaxed, with that half-sleepy relaxation that comes with a good meal and good company.

'What is it you would really like to do with your radio show? Is it just entertainment? Or information and debate? Or do you have some ambition for what you could achieve with talk-back?'

'I have this vague idea,' he replied quietly and

slowly, 'of being some sort of...well, mender of destinies, I suppose.'

'What *do* you mean?'

'I mean that many of the people who ring on the open line to tell me their stories seem to be not in their right niche, to be treading paths which are not theirs, solely because they are not aware...'

Roman paused to sip his coffee and to stare at some unseen horizon. Then he continued. 'Yes...in a manner of speaking I would like that...to be a mender of destinies by helping people to change direction.'

'You mean by giving them advice?'

'No, just by listening and talking. I know that I'm not exceptionally intelligent, but perhaps a mender of destinies doesn't need exceptional intelligence? Perhaps what I need is to be able to see into the lives of all sorts of people and—at least in my imagination—get myself inside their minds.'

There was a long, heavy silence, and then Roman continued.

'I don't often talk like this. I don't even dare think about it too much or I'd start laughing at myself. After all, I'm just a former disc-jockey who hosts a late-night radio talk-back show. And I became that almost by accident.'

'Sometimes good things happen by accident,' said Hugh.

At three o'clock Roman excused himself. 'I want to be out at the airport by a quarter to four,' he explained.

'Someone arriving?' asked Hugh.

'Raffael Escobar is due to fly in then.'

'The great man himself. And are you going to meet him?'

147

'Hardly,' said Roman with a chuckle. 'I just want to be there. I'd like to see him up close.'

Roman's drive to the airport was made easy by the light Sunday traffic, and by the cool air that had turned a heatwave into a comfortable late spring temperature.

By the time the car was parked Roman had to hurry to be at the International Terminal by three forty five. As it turned out, he needn't have worried. The Continental flight had touched down on time but there were the usual delays with baggage and customs clearance.

Behind the roped-off area outside the door from the customs hall, there was, as always, a large and ethnically diverse crowd waiting to meet friends and relations. It was a rather sterile, echoing area, and Roman began to pace up and down, impatient to catch a glimpse of the man who had precipitated this whole drama.

Then, quite suddenly, there he was.

He was unmistakable: there was the high, noble forehead, the black hair swept straight back, the dark, deep-set eyes, the pointed, and very Spanish, beard. He was taller than Roman had anticipated, and his calm, unlined face made him look younger than his years.

Roman pressed up against the barrier, and Raffael Escobar passed close by him, close enough to reach out and touch. There was a vivid and burning light, a kind of fearful energy and life, in Escobar's eyes, but his mouth was grim and set, and his manner earnest and purposeful. Roman remembered Michelle Thomas's description: meeting Escobar was like meeting royalty or a powerful president.

To Roman's right, where the barrier ended, Raffael Escobar was greeted by Tyler Davis. Words passed between the two that Roman could not hear. Presumably words of sympathy to begin with, and then dealing with practical matters: luggage, transport to the city, accommodation.

For a moment Roman glanced away, and when he looked back Escobar and Davis had been joined by a third figure. The third man had his back to Roman, so his identity was not immediately clear. Then he turned to greet Escobar, showing his profile, and it was Simon Miller!

For a long moment Simon and his father just looked at each other, then some words were exchanged. And finally, Escobar threw an arm around Simon's shoulder and hugged his son. From what he knew of the family history Roman expected Simon to pull away, to recoil, to reject this fatherly approach. He did not. He seemed, from where Roman was standing some distance away, to welcome his father's affection.

Then the two of them, with Tyler Davis tagging along behind carrying a suitcase, walked together out of the airport with arms around each other's shoulders.

Roman walked slowly back to the car park, puzzled; puzzled by Raffael Escobar's great affection for his long estranged son; puzzled by Simon's welcome of that affection.

After nibbling a scratch meal at his apartment, Roman drove back to St Thomas' for the evening service still wearing his puzzlement like a heavy overcoat. He knew himself well enough to know that he was not consumed by ambition, but by curiosity about his fellow human beings. And that afternoon's behaviour at the airport was as curious and inexplicable as any that Roman had ever known.

The Sunday evening meeting at St Thomas' was a highlight of Roman's week. For a start, many of the people he met there he counted as friends. Secondly, at St Thomas' he was not a radio star, just a person. And thirdly, he found Hugh Marsden's preaching to be the kind of on-going education that kept him growing as a person.

That night, however, he found it harder than usual to give his whole attention to the meeting. At the back of his mind, like a shadow flitting down an alleyway, was this haunting idea that Simon's behaviour was the key to the whole mystery surrounding the murder of Salvador Escobar.

Hugh was doing a series of sermons on 'competing world views'. Using the work of writers such as Francis Schaeffer and James Sire he was contrasting the Christian world view with the competing materialistic and pantheistic world views. Hugh explained that world view was the English translation of a German word—*weltanschauung*—and it meant a philosophy of life, or, perhaps, a mental picture or map of what the world is like and how it works. And everyone has one of these world views, not just professors of philosophy but truck drivers and shop assistants too, because all human beings have their own mental picture of what the world is like and how it works. It was part of being human.

The interesting question is: how do people's world views change?

Roman believed that Simon's world view had changed dramatically in the course of less than a week. But what had changed it? Was it something Salvador had said before he died? Or was it the murder of Salvador itself that had made the difference?

If you woke up one morning, thought Roman, to the realisation that you had committed a murder, then surely you would look at the world very differently?

Roman wondered if it was Simon's guilt that had changed him so dramatically. And, if not his guilt, then what?

Hugh was explaining from the pulpit that the only way to test the truth, or falsity, of a world view was to 'live within it'. And more than that, to live critically within it. One could live unthinkingly with a materialistic world view, but as soon as one started living in an aware and critical way with a materialistic world view it led to profound despair and a lack of purpose or direction.

Roman knew from experience that the only way to understand, let alone test, the Christian world view was to trust oneself to it, and live within it: to live as if it were true and discover from within the difference it makes...

This business of shifting perspectives, of shifting world views, could, he realised, be the key to the puzzle he was struggling with.

After the meeting, Roman hung around, as he always did, for an hour or so of coffee and conversation. But on this particular Sunday he was distracted and unable to give his full attention to his friends.

'What are you doing for Christmas, Mark?' someone asked.

'Ah, going up to Coffs Harbour—that's where my father lives these days—my sisters and their families will be coming down from Brisbane and we'll have a big, old-fashioned family Christmas,' he replied, and explained to a newcomer that his father was a retired bank manager. But his mind was elsewhere.

The conversation wandered on to what other people were doing for Christmas, and in his distracted frame of mind, Roman was more comfortable as a listener than as a participant.

Eventually the coffee ran out, the company broke up, and Roman drove back home.

That night, just as he was falling asleep, the pieces fell into place. Without any particular warning he suddenly realised that he was inside the puzzle looking out, and not outside looking in. He could understand exactly what had happened and why. He could see the place of even small apparently irrelevant items in the scheme of things; they fitted in and they made sense.

Tomorrow he would have to do something about it.

Chapter 9

Roman awoke in the morning knowing exactly what he was going to do. While he slept his sub-conscious had wrestled with the problem, had identified a weak link, and had come up with a plan of action.

He went through his usual morning routine like a robot, his mind pre-occupied with the day ahead. When breakfast was over he checked the time: it was still too early to put his plan into action. He was too restless to fill the intervening time with preparations for Monday night's show, so he locked up and walked downstairs to McDougall Street.

Often Roman's brain worked best when his legs were moving, and as he walked slowly down McDougall Street and across the road to Milson's Park he again went over his plans for the day.

At this time on a Monday morning he had the park to himself. The tops of the tall palm trees in the centre of the park were moving gently in a soft sea breeze blowing off the harbour.

Roman turned towards Careening Cove, watching

the sun glinting off the waves as he walked. At the water's edge he found a small pebble in the grass, and threw it in a low, flat arc across the water, making it skip twice over the waves before it sank. It was exactly what he used to do as a child.

Glancing at his watch he saw that it was time. He had no idea if his plan would work, but he had to try.

Roman drove to Shirley Road, Wollstonecraft, and turned the corner into Cable Street. He did a U-turn and parked the car just back from the corner, partially concealed by a gum tree. From here he could observe the Miller house without, he hoped, being seen himself.

For some time he sat in the car watching the house. No movement could be seen. No one left or entered, not a curtain flickered.

Roman picked up his car phone and dialled Network Systems.

'Network Systems. Good morning, can I help you?'

Roman recognised the voice of Naomi Parker the receptionist. Giving his voice a gravelly edge that he hoped would disguise it Roman said, 'May I speak to Mr Simon Miller please?'

'Certainly, sir. Hold the line please.'

There were several clicks and a short delay, and then Simon's voice came on the line.

'Hello?'

As soon as he heard that voice Roman hung up.

So, Simon had gone back to work. That meant that only Liz and Bertram were in the house opposite.

Roman picked up the car phone again. This time he rang the Miller's home number. When he heard it start to ring, Roman imagined the telephone ringing in the small dining room—the breakfast room Bertram had called it—in the big, ramshackle old house opposite.

154

The phone rang for several minutes before it was answered. 'Hello?'

'Liz, is that you? It's Mark Roman calling.'

'Oh, Mark. I'm so relieved to hear your voice. Ever since this horrible business started I've never known what phone calls to expect.'

'Have the media been bothering you?'

'Since yesterday they have. When the police released the name of the victim to the media they started calling up everyone who worked at Network Systems to plague them with questions. Simon, very sensibly, has refused to speak to them.'

'I'm sorry to hear that you've been pestered,' said Roman, who sometimes felt embarrassed by the media, as though he should feel responsible because he worked in the industry.

'We've coped,' said Liz, with weary resignation.

'The reason for this call,' explained Roman, 'is because I'd like to see you for a private chat.'

'Well look, I'm just on my way out to do the weekly shopping—I do it every Monday morning when the shops are less crowded. And I really do have to go since the refrigerator is looking fairly empty. Perhaps you could come over when I get back?'

'I want this to be a very private conversation Liz, just you and me. I think I'd prefer it if we met somewhere other than your house.'

'Oh...I see...Well, that's all right, I suppose,' said Liz hesitantly.

'Where do you do your shopping?'

'At Woolworths at Crows Nest.'

'That's in Falcon Street isn't it?'

'Yes, that's the one.'

'Next door to Woolworths, right along side it in

155

Falcon Street, is a coffee shop and gelato bar called "Bravo"—do you know it?'

'Oh yes, I've walked past it often.'

'Why don't I meet you there when you've finished your shopping?'

'All right . . . all right, if you want to.'

'Now, when will you finish your shopping? When can we meet?'

'What's the time now? It's nearly ten o'clock. My shopping usually takes about an hour, so if I leave now I should be finished by eleven.'

'Fine. How about meeting me at the Bravo at eleven?'

'All right, Mark. I'll get started straight away, and I'll meet you at the Bravo in Falcon Street at eleven o'clock.'

'Just one other thing, Liz,' said Roman, 'There's a quick job I have to do between now and then, so if I'm a few minutes late will you wait for me?'

'Yes, that's all right. If you're not there right on the hour I can order a cup of coffee and wait for you.'

'That's terrific Liz. I'll see you then.'

Roman replaced the car phone in its holder, and sat very still watching the Miller house, diagonally opposite and partially hidden by the intervening gum leaves.

Several minutes later an elderly Corolla pulled out of the Miller driveway and chugged up the street. When he was certain that it was out of sight, Roman got out of the Volvo, locked the car door behind him, and walked across the road to the Miller place.

After ringing the door bell he had to wait on the front porch for a long time. Roman began to worry that Bertram was still in bed. Or perhaps he was so deaf he couldn't hear the bell? Or perhaps he just never answered the door when Liz wasn't home?

Roman's fears turned out to be groundless when his lengthy wait came to an end with the click of locks and the opening of the front door.

'Oh!' said a startled Bertram. 'It's you, Mr Roman. I'm afraid Liz is not here. In fact, you've just missed her.'

'It's not Liz I've come to see, Bertram,' said Roman, 'It's you.'

'Me? I'm afraid that I can't help you, Mr Roman. You come back when Liz is here.' And he started to close the door.

Roman stepped forward and put his hand firmly against it.

'I would really like to have a chat with you, Bertram,' he said in the friendliest, least threatening voice he could manage, 'a private chat—just the two of us.'

'Well. . .I don't know. . .'

'It will only take a few minutes. I'll be gone long before Liz gets back.'

'I can't really tell you anything. . .you understand,' said the old man. 'I don't know anything.'

'Just one or two small things you might be able to help with,' persisted Roman. 'Please.'

'I suppose it's all right then. . .you might as well come in.'

Bertram swung the door fully open and stepped back to allow Roman to enter. He led the way down the hall to the small sitting room that Roman had visited twice before.

'Would you like a cup of tea, Mr Roman?'

'No thank you, Bertram.'

'Good. I sometimes burn myself when I try to work the kettle. My hands are not as steady as they used to be.'

'You and I have not had much of a chance to talk, have we?' said Roman, settling himself in an armchair.

'What do you mean?' asked Bertram, as he perched nervously on the edge of the sofa.

'Oh, just that I've had some long chats with Liz. And with Simon. But so far you and I have only passed the time of day as it were.'

'I suppose so.'

'And so it struck me that a chat between you and me is somewhat overdue.'

'A chat about what?'

'About the murder of Salvador Escobar.'

'I can't tell you anything about that,' said Bertram, his eyes darting nervously about the room as he spoke, as if he was looking for a way of escape.

'Can't? Or won't?'

'Eh?'

'Is it that you can't tell me anything about the murder, Bertram, or that you won't?'

'I can't. I just can't. I don't know anything.'

'Well there you are lying to me, Bertram,' said Roman in a weary voice. 'When you say you don't know anything I'm very much afraid that you are lying to me.'

'No, no I'm not! You shouldn't be talking to me. You should talk to Liz, not to me.'

'But you are the one who knows, Bertram. And the one who can tell the truth—if you choose to.'

'No, I can't. I can't say anything.'

Roman stood up and walked over to the window. He was tall and broad-shouldered, and to Bertram he seemed to loom over him, like some giant, menacing shadow. As he stood looking out of the window it seemed to Bertram that he blocked out all of the sunlight.

'I understand that you are afraid,' said Roman without turning around to face the old man. 'I understand that you can't speak because you are afraid to speak.'

All that Bertram Miller could see of Mark Roman was his back, a broad expanse of back, large and solid and immovable.

'I don't know what you mean,' quavered the old man. 'What do you mean?'

'Of course,' continued Roman, as if Bertram had not spoken, 'it may no longer feel like fear. You have lived with it for so long now that you may be unaware of how afraid you are.'

'You'll have to go now,' said Bertram, and he started to rise from the sofa as he spoke.

'Sit down!' snapped Roman, turning back from the window to face the man in the old brown cardigan. There was an anger in Roman's voice that shocked Bertram, and although the command to 'sit down' was not shouted—or even said very loudly—it seemed to echo around the house. Bertram found himself unable to disobey, and he meekly lowered himself back down onto the sofa.

'You see, Bertram, I know what happened,' said Roman, advancing forward and towering over the old man like some mighty oak tree.

Bertram did not reply, he just looked up at Roman, his mouth agape, his breath coming in heavy wheezes.

The silence in the room was as heavy as a blanket and as oppressive as a heatwave.

Roman walked back to his armchair and sat down again. 'I know what happened,' he repeated.

Still the old man did not respond.

Roman was suddenly aware of how thirsty he was, but having come this far he dare not break the atmosphere by asking for a drink. He licked his parched lips and continued. 'Parts of it I have guessed, but most of it I know, Bertram—I really know.'

'You can't,' replied Bertram Miller. It was almost a whisper, and he seemed to be speaking more to himself than to Roman.

'Believe me, Bertram—I know. And very soon the police will know. That's why I think it would be better if you were to tell me everything now, first, before I go to the police.'

Roman looked directly at Bertram. They made eye-to-eye contact, and Roman recognised the glazed, confused look of a frightened old man.

'What are you frightened of, Bertram?' asked Roman, in his gentle soft-sell voice. 'Are you frightened of the police? Are you frightened of prison? Are you frightened of Liz? What is it that bothers you most, Bertram?'

Instead of replying the old man just stared, blinking rapidly, like a wounded animal at bay.

'I'd like you to tell me, Bertram—I'd like you to confirm what I already know. Will you do that?'

There was a very long and painful silence. As the seconds ticked away Roman was aware of the sounds of the house: the barely perceptible whoosh of the southerly winds under the eaves; the faintest of creaks as the old house shifted and settled by a millimetre or two; the distant ticking of a clock in the hall.

'Yes. I'll tell you,' muttered the old man in a hoarse whisper.

'It was Liz who murdered Salvador Escobar, wasn't it, Bertram?'

'Yes, yes, it was Liz.'

'On Thursday some time she rang the office didn't she, the office of Network Systems, and she made an

160

appointment to see young Escobar didn't she?'

'Yes . . . she did.'

'And she went there that evening and spoke to Escobar, and when he wouldn't do what she wanted, she killed him, didn't she?'

'Yes,' muttered Bertram, looking down at the carpet, not daring to raise his eyes to meet Roman's.

'And your job was to be an accessory, wasn't it Bertram? An accessory before the fact is what the law calls it. Your job was to manufacture the alibi, wasn't it?'

This time he didn't reply, but merely nodded. Roman leaned forward to look closely at the old man and was surprised to see a single tear catching the light as it rolled down a groove in that furrowed face between the nose and the cheek.

'Her appointment to see Escobar was for when?' asked Roman.

'For half past six.'

'So he was fitting her in between his appointments with Simon and with me. She went there expecting only to meet a representative from head office in Ecuador, is that right?'

'No—she knew it was Salvador Escobar she was meeting.'

'How did she know?'

'He had introduced himself on the telephone—when she rang to ask for an appointment.'

'And by so doing he signed his death warrant.'

'I suppose so,' replied Bertram quietly.

'So when she left this house she knew who she was going to meet?'

'Yes.'

'And she knew she was going to kill him?'

'No! Only if she had to.'

'If he wouldn't fall in with her plans?'

'Yes.'

'And what were her plans?'

'To keep Simon away from his father. At all costs, Simon must not be allowed to come into contact with his father.' Bertram sounded as if he was repeating a lesson learned off by rote.

No doubt, thought Roman, he had heard Liz use those words often enough to have them imprinted on his mind.

'But Salvador would not go along with Liz?' persisted Roman.

'No,' said the old man quietly. 'No. He insisted that his one goal in life was to bring Simon and his father back together again. He was very foolish. Liz told me she tried to reason with him. But he wouldn't listen. It was like a campaign with him, like a crusade. So he had to die. You do understand that Mr Roman, don't you?'

'I am beginning to understand,' replied Roman.

'And so she killed him,' muttered Bertram, more to himself than to Roman. 'She killed him.'

'She didn't use the weapon she had taken with her, did she?' asked Roman. 'She used weapons that she found in the office?'

'Yes, that's right. She said the weapons couldn't be traced back to us that way. She's very clever is my Liz.'

'So she hit Escobar over the head to immobilise him, then she picked up a letter-opener and stabbed him, didn't she?'

'She didn't know that it was Simon's letter-opener that she used,' muttered the old man.

'I'm sure she didn't. That was just bad luck on her part. And she was still in the building when I arrived?'

'Yes. She told me that she heard you come in the

162

lift, and so she left via the stairs.'

'And when I telephoned here you did your part, you created the alibi by using the radio-cassette player that I saw next to the telphone to play a tape that Liz had recorded in which she said that she was in the kitchen and couldn't come to the phone.'

'Yes,' said the old man, his brows knitting in puzzlement. 'But how do you know, Mr Roman, how do you know all this?'

'In the first place when I spoke to Liz on the phone late on the night of the murder—when the identity of the murdered man had not been released—she said something very strange. After saying that Simon suffered from deep-seated trauma from his mother's death she said: "What will happen next? Will his brother be murdered?" And I wondered why the brother should come up at all. It seemed to me that Liz was revealing more knowledge than she should have had.'

'I see,' muttered Bertram quietly.

'Then secondly that alibi phone-call bothered me. I could hear every word that Liz was saying quite clearly. Of course I could, since what I was hearing was a tape cassette player right next to the phone. But over the next few days I noticed several times that when someone called out from another room, I, on the other end of the phone, could not make out what they were saying. And of course I saw the radio-cassette player here, right beside the telephone.'

'Ah, yes,' murmured Bertram.

'And there was the nature of the wounds. Why was Escobar knocked out before he was stabbed? It occurred to me that Liz is a small woman and the only way she could stab a strong young man without being beaten off would be if that young man was unconscious.'

'She hit him from behind,' said Bertram, 'and then stabbed him when he was lying unconscious across the desk.'

'And Liz would have had the anatomical knowledge to know exactly where to thrust the knife because when she was much younger she was a nurse. I discovered that from the photographs displayed in this room.'

'Yes, Liz was nursing when we met. She gave it up when we got married.'

'Those clues pointed me towards Liz as the murderer. For some time I remained puzzled because I couldn't see the motive. I was only when I realised that this was Liz's *second* murder that I understood.'

'So. . .you know about that too?'

'Some of it I know, and some I've guessed. I know that Liz murdered her sister Peggy sixteen years ago by poisoning her with nicotine. Liz's nursing background would also have given her knowledge of the poisonous qualities of nicotine. A sufficiently poisonous concentrate of nicotine can be obtained simply by boiling down the contents of ordinary cigarettes. And sixteen years ago Liz was a smoker, giving her daily access to the material she needed to make her poison.'

Bertram did not say anything, he just slouched lower in his chair looking frightened and dejected.

'And although she gave up smoking ten years ago,' continued Roman, 'she bought a whole carton of cigarettes just recently. I know because the empty carton spilled out of the garbage can yesterday when Simon kicked it in anger. And that made me think: if she killed the first time with nicotine poison, was that how she planned to kill the second time?'

'Yes. . .yes it was.'

'Did she distil another poisonous concentrate of nicotine from that carton of cigarettes?'

'Yes. She made me help her. We did it out in the laundry, just in case there were splashes and stains.'

'And did she take that nicotine with her when she met with Salvador Escobar?'

'Yes. The plan was that if he was unco-operative Liz would suggest that they have some coffee—every office has coffee making facilities—and then look for an opportunity to slip the nicotine into Escobar's coffee.'

'But when she saw the heavy glass paperweight,' said Roman, 'she changed her mind, didn't she?'

'Yes. When she came back home she was very pleased with herself. She said the weapons could never be traced back to us because they were objects that belonged in the office.'

'And there was always a risk that nicotine poisoning could link this murder with the death of Peggy sixteen years ago, wasn't there?'

'I said that to Liz,' said Bertram, his head shaking from side to side as he spoke. 'I said that. She said not to worry. But when she got into the office she took my advice and used another weapon. She took my advice about that, Mr Roman, she took my advice.'

'I imagine that she doesn't often take your advice, does she Bertram?'

'Not often, Mr Roman, not often.'

'So tell me about that first murder, all those years ago in Ecuador. I imagine she was jealous of her sister?'

'She hated her,' said Bertram, looking up abruptly and staring straight into Roman's eyes. 'She hated Peggy with a fierce hatred. Peggy was always the good looking one, and the clever one at school, and the popular one. They were always competing those sisters, and Peggy always won. She even got married before Liz, the older sister. And she made a much better match than Liz. I was never much of a catch, Mr Roman. I think Liz only married me to prove to Peggy that she could catch a man too. And then Peggy had children and Liz. . .well. . .the doctors all said that Liz couldn't.'

'So Liz killed her?'

'Yes.'

'And stole the little boy she was unable to have herself?'

'But she really did love Simon, Mr Roman, you must believe that.'

'Love? I'm not sure about that, Bertram. It looks like a pretty selfish sort of love to me. She cut that young boy off from his father by accusing his father of a murder that she herself had committed!'

The old man did not respond. Slowly his head sagged forward until his shoulders were bowed and his face resting in his hands. He said nothing.

'But there's one thing I still don't understand,' continued Roman. 'How did she get the young Simon—five or six or whatever age he was—to say that he had seen his father put something into his mother's coffee?'

'Oh, that?' said Bertram softly, without looking up. 'Simon had misbehaved the day before and his father had punished him. He knew he was telling a lie, and he did it to get back at his father. Besides which Liz was always whispering in his ear about how wonderful Australia was, and how happy he would be living with us in Australia. She made it sound like living in Disneyland. He was easily tempted.'

'So Liz poisoned the sister she had hated for years,

accused Raffael Escobar of the murder and then—with that excuse—fled to Australia with Simon?'

'Yes. She had finally defeated the sister who had always done better than her, and she had the child that she had always hungered for.'

'But there's still more to the story than that, isn't there Bertram?' persisted Roman.

'What do you mean?'

'I mean that there is also the character of Raffael Escobar to be considered.'

Bertram buried his head in his hands and did not respond.

'Raffael Escobar is exactly the opposite to the poisonous, and lying, character sketch of him that Liz gave me the first time we met. He is the exact reverse of all the things she claimed about him. He loved his son with an undying love and fought for him through the courts. When that failed I believe—from what I have learned of Raffael Escobar's character—he would have insisted on providing for his estranged son's welfare. And in fact, I believe he did.'

'What do you mean?'

'Despite the loss of Liz's family wealth and all the inherited assets—apart from this house—despite that, as I say, I found in this very room evidence of substantial shareholdings. While continuing to lie to Simon and to the world about the character of Raffael Escobar, Liz accepted the money he sent to provide for Simon, and used that money to invest for herself. That's true, isn't it Bertram?'

The old man opened his mouth to speak and then just nodded dumbly.

'That most remarkable thing to come out of this whole story,' resumed Roman, 'is the character of Raffael Escobar. His young son lied and supported the false accusation of murder against him, and then, succumbing to temptation, willingly fled with his aunt to Australia. In court cases lasting several years young Simon's testimony was consistently one of rejecting his father and expressing a desire to live with his aunt. And as an adult he continued to reject his father's advances. But Raffael Escobar never stopped loving his son. In the end he sent his elder son, Salvador, to restore the relationship with Simon, the lost son. It is a remarkable story, isn't it Bertram?'

The old man did not respond, he did not speak, he did not even nod in agreement.

'And it was Raffael Escobar's persistence,' said Roman, 'that threw Liz into such a panic. If Simon's contact with his father was ever restored he would discover that his beloved aunt had been lying to him all these years. And Liz would have lost her nephew—her adopted son—her prize possession, her one triumph over the departed sister she hated. Simon was hers, and she was determined to hang on to him at any cost. Furthermore, if Simon was restored to his father it would only be a matter of time before her theft of money intended for Simon would be uncovered, and that would not only further anger Simon, it might lead to a criminal charge.'

The old man listened but did not respond in any way.

Roman continued. 'So Liz had to keep Simon and his father apart. She kept pressing him to resign from Network Systems, and insisted that he ignore his father's letters. And then, when she heard that someone was arriving from head office she panicked: she contacted me in an attempt to persuade Simon to resign quickly; and she rang the office to contact this head office representative—presumably to try to persuade or bribe him to leave Simon alone and pass on no messages from Raffael. To her horror when she rang the office she discovered that the representative was Simon's own brother. She went to meet him intending to plead with him to leave Simon alone, and, if he refused, to kill him. That, she reasoned, would end any chance of Simon being restored to his father, and might even have persuaded Simon to leave the company.'

'Liz is very clever you know,' Bertram said, in a faint and vague voice. 'Very clever is my Liz, very clever.'

'Not clever enough,' said Roman quietly. 'Not this time.' Roman stood up again and began to pace up and down the small floor space of the sitting room.

'Now, Bertram,' he said as he paced, 'there is something I want you to do for me.'

'What?'

'I want you to come with me, and I want you to tell someone else the story you've just told me.'

'Go? Go where? Tell who?'

'The police.'

'No! No, I couldn't do that!'

'You've danced to Liz's tune for the whole of your married life, Bertram, frightened of how she would react to the slightest opposition. But this is too important for you to simply go on doing what you are told to do. You have a responsibility, Bertram.'

'No! It wasn't my idea. And I didn't do it.'

'But you helped. The law will call it being an accessory before the fact. You will serve time in prison, Bertram—unless, of course, you help the police by coming with me now and telling them everything you know.'

Bertram's eyes opened wider and Roman thought he was winning the old man over. But he was wrong. 'No! No, I can't do it!'

Roman glanced at his wrist-watch. It was ten past eleven. Assuming that Liz had sat down in Bravo's at eleven he was not sure how long he could count on her waiting for his non-appearance. Might she already be driving back to the house?'

'Bertram,' he said sternly. 'You're not young, and you're not well: do you really want to go to prison?'

'I don't think I could . . .' said the old man with an involuntary shudder.

'You must face up to the fact that murder cannot be ignored. The police and the courts will not treat your role lightly. But if you come forward with information that may just help your case.'

'But I shouldn't. What will Liz think?'

'Liz has murdered twice. If she is cornered and frightened she may kill again.'

'Liz frightens me,' said Bertram quietly.

'She frightens me too,' said Roman. 'Please, Bertram, help me stop her. She can be put out of harm's way.'

The old man seemed to be thinking.

'Please, Bertram, please,' pleaded Roman in his most persuasive voice.

There was a moment of suspended time as Roman waited for a response. Then, Bertram nodded his head. He didn't speak, he just nodded.

'Come along then Bertram,' said Roman urgently. 'We must go now, immediately, before Liz gets back.'

That suggestion motivated the old man to start moving. 'Yes,' he said. 'Before Liz gets back.'

Even so Roman found it painfully slow getting Bertram Miller to his feet, shuffling down the hall, opening the front door and locking it behind them.

Roman kept glancing up the street expecting Liz's Corolla to arrive at any moment as he led Bertram across the road to the parked Volvo. Bertram seemed to have fallen into a kind of a daze as Roman settled him into the front passenger's seat and fastened his seat belt.

Once Roman was seated behind the wheel and had the engine running he breathed a sigh of relief: he felt for the first time that they were really going to make it.

He drove out of Cable Street, turned right into Shirley Road, and right again at the top of the street towards the Pacific Highway. As they rounded that corner Roman saw Liz in the Corolla pass them going the other way. He glanced at his passenger, but Bertram, his eyes half closed and his head nodding, had seen nothing.

What would Liz do when she arrived home and found Bertram missing? Would she panic? Start a search? Or did Bertram sometimes wander off on harmless walks on his own? Would she call the police and report him missing? Or might she guess what Roman was doing?

At the highway, Roman turned south, and parked in a loading zone opposite the North Sydney police station.

Then he had to go through the painfully slow business of getting the old man out of the car, leading him in his slow, shuffling walk down to the traffic lights, and across the street.

Inside the police station Roman approached the uniformed officer at the front desk. 'Would Detective Kline or Detective Fitzpatrick be available, please?'

'One moment, sir, I'll find out. Who shall I say is calling?'

'Mark Roman.'

'Oh yes, so it is. I like your radio show, Mr Roman.'

A few moments later Detective Jim Kline came to

the front desk. 'Morning, Mr Roman. What can I do for you?'

'Mr Kline, allow me to introduce Bertram Miller: he has something to tell you.'

Chapter 10

Roman never saw Liz Miller again, except on television during her court appearances. Somehow, he noticed, she always managed to look like a woman wronged. The world, she seemed to be saying, should be more understanding and forgiving of what she had done.

Her lawyers pleaded not guilty and fought the case by challenging the prosecution's evidence at every point. But the message that Roman read on Liz's face, whenever he caught a glimpse of it in the newspapers or on the television news, seemed to convey a different message: 'I did it, and I was justified in doing it.'

She was found guilty and sentenced to a lengthy term of imprisonment. Her lawyers filed appeals against both the verdict and the sentence. Eventually, after the wheels of justice had turned in their slow but inevitable circles, both appeals were lost.

Sometimes at night during his talk-back radio show Roman thought of Liz in a prison farm on the edge of Sydney, and he wondered if she had a radio and if she was listening to his show.

Bertram died quietly in his sleep, from a stroke, shortly after giving evidence at the preliminary committal hearing. This evidence given before the magistrate was, because Bertram had died, later read into evidence at Liz's murder trial. It played a key role in convicting her. Perhaps it was Bertram's final comment on their years of marriage.

Simon remained in Sydney until all the trials and appeals were over, and then he moved to Ecuador to live and work with his father. While he was still in Sydney Roman had only one contact with him—a letter in which Simon thanked him for his role in, as he put it, shedding light in a dark corner. In that letter he described very movingly how he had asked his father to forgive him and accept him back into the family, and how Raffael Escobar had wept over the returning prodigal.

Two years later Roman had his last contact with Simon Miller, or Simon Escobar as he now preferred to be know. It was a letter from Quito, Ecuador, describing Simon's life and work with his father. In that second letter was one phrase, one simple four-word phrase, Roman found unforgettable. He kept the letter, and occasionally he would pull it out of a drawer to read it again, knowing that his heart would be strangely warmed within him as he read Simon's words:

I have come home.

The Key to the Allegory

The Second Death is an allegory—that is, a story with
two levels of meaning.

You may prefer to work out for yourself the deeper
meaning represented by the characters in the story,
or. . .you can read the following page on which the
second meaning of the story is explained. (The page
can be read by holding it up to a mirror.)

WARNING

Do not read the following page until after you
have read the book!

Simon Miller: represents you and me; he is a pilgrim on the journey that we all take from this world to the next.

Liz and Bertram Miller: represent two sides (the active and the passive) of our fallen human nature that alienates us from God, corrupts our understanding, and acts as a barrier between us and God.

Raffael Escobar: The father—represents God who perseveres in loving us and refusing to abandon us despite our wilful rebellion against him.

Salvador Escobar: The son sent by the father—represents Jesus Christ, who by his death (at the hands of our corrupt and evil human nature) reconciles us to God the Father.

And we have seen and tell others that the Father sent his Son to be the Saviour of the world.[1] Through the Son, then, God decided to bring the whole universe back to himself. God made peace through his Son's sacrificial death on the cross . . .[2] For God loved the world so much that he gave his only Son, so that everyone who believes in him may not die but have eternal life.[3]

– The Good News Bible

1 – 1 John 4:14; 2 – Colossians 1:20; 3 – John 3:16.